Wesley turned on him, no longer restraining his anger. "Are you *trying* to turn every possible clue into goo? What on earth is the matter with you?"

"I was trying to stop him, not kill him," Angel said, emotion thrumming against his soul like the heartbeat he no longer had. Once released, it didn't ease . . . didn't ebb into the night as it should have. No respite here.

Gunn ran to where the demon had been, grabbing up the ax. "Doesn't look like you did *either*. If this particular demon had one of those odd stone things, it doesn't have one anymore."

"That's what his companion was after?" Wesley asked.

"If it had anything to be after at all—besides us," Angel said, and shrugged, so much more casual on the outside than on the in.

"Well, we can't *ask* him, can we?" Wesley said. "We can't ask *either* of them."

Angel stopped, blocking Wesley's path. "Let it go, Wesley," he said softly. Dangerously.

Angel™

Available from Simon Pulse and Pocket Books

ANGEL ™

impressions

Doranna Durgin

An original novel based on the television series
created by Joss Whedon & David Greenwalt

SIMON PULSE

New York London Toronto Sydney Singapore

Historian's Note: This story takes place during the third season of *Angel*.

First Simon Pulse edition February 2003
Text copyright © 2003 Twentieth Century Fox Inc.
All Rights Reserved.

SIMON PULSE
An imprint of Simon & Schuster
Children's Publishing Division
1230 Avenue of the Americas
New York, NY 10020

The text of this book was set in New Caledonia.

Printed in the United States of America
10 9 8 7 6 5 4 3 2 1

Library of Congress Control Number 2002113626
ISBN 0-7434-2758-0

With thanks to many people, because one never writes a book in a vacuum. Jennifer didn't let me get away with anything, and Amy applied her Angelometer, and Lisa and Micol put up with me on the editorial end. The SFF gang cheered my snippets, and Ruth, Kevin, and Kristina offered up demon names (Veroscini, Khundarr, and Slith, respectively). Tom and my family were cheerleaders (I love e-mail), and Google was my first research stop. (I love the Web!) The Los Angeles Zoo was kind enough to send me an entire PR kit full of info, so if I got anything wrong it's entirely my fault. And of course the dogs all did their best to be as distracting as possible, which is their job. This book is for all of you!

CHAPTER ONE

In one reality . . .

A young Tuingas demon moved respectfully through the special pocket universe it was his honor to maintain. He was slightly small for his clan, but endowed with the usual assortment of limbs and quite a masculine long-nose that he liked to drape back over his shoulder in an affected habit. He said it kept his long-nose out of the dust he often raised while tending the less frequently visited family shrines, but in what served as his heart even he knew that he merely liked tossing the long-nose around.

The demon moved from one family shrine to another within the pocket dimension created and sustained by his people. At this shrine he checked his protective amulet, buffing it slightly against his leathery skin. Only family members and highly trained priests could withstand the presence of the deathstones without amulet protection, and this particular deathstone was newly arrived, potent not only in its freshness, but because of the demon from which it had come. One of their warriors, and a great hero. His deathstone was a handsome one, a solid fist-sized oblong with unusually consistent color and texture. A stone the outside world could never fully appreciate . . . or even survive.

Reassured by the amulet's icy response to his touch, the demon entered the marble-walled shrine, pulling a little red wagon liberated from the human world. As fresh as it was, this shrine would need little in the way of maintenance; he rummaged through the contents of the wagon and withdrew a bright yellow feather duster. Humming a nasal tune through both face-nose and long-nose at once, he applied the duster with enthusiasm, sweeping clean the empty stone nooks and crannies that would hold future deathstones for this now-exalted family, and working in toward the single occupied central pedestal. With the wagon trailing behind him, he bent over to pluck a gum wrapper from the plush shag rug, not the least bit annoyed when his long-nose fell forward. After all, it merely offered him another chance to toss it back over his shoulder.

But he neglected to put aside the feather duster when he reached for his long-nose. In fact, he all but jammed the feather duster up his long-nose in a painful collision that at first seemed to have no particular consequence. He stood mildly stunned, long-nose smarting, his dull black little eyes watering, when he felt the first tingling warning way at the back of both noses. Frantically, he patted down his broad waist belt in search of tissues, horrified at the thought of a sneeze—a *doublesneeze*—in this quiet, sacred space.

The doublesneeze rose in an inevitable wave of nose-spasm, violent enough to bend him in half. He lost his balance, staggered backward, and—*oh horror*—found himself caught in a second spasm, a double doublesneeze right here in the hero's shrine. He fell, kicking the wagon in one direction while his arms windmilled in the other and his head fetched up against something hard.

He lay stunned.

After a moment he whimpered, opened his gummy little eyes, and pulled himself upright. His wagon and his supplies had tipped over, but to his great relief the red paint had not marred any of the marble walls. He heaved a great thankful sigh and crawled over to it, set it upright, and reached for the spilled supplies.

Only then did he realize that the lump on the back of his head had been raised by the warrior's deathstone pedestal.

Only then did he realize the deathstone was gone, propelled by a conjunction of magics never meant to make physical contact with one another. Gone from its pedestal, from this shrine, from this pocket dimension. Gone to the outside world, where it would wreak destruction.

Gone to Los Angeles.

In another, more familiar reality . . .

A small rat-like demon clung to the edge of the roof, leaning out over the five-story drop to peer down at the rattling fire escape. "Here!" it squeaked, accidentally spitting in its fear—although its extreme overbite made a certain amount of spitting inevitable in any case. "Take the purse, take it!" It flung a floppy crocheted purse down at its pursuer on the fire escape. "You don't have enough problems in this city, you gotta pick on a little guy like me?" And with an agitated twitch, it scampered off across the flat roof.

The man on the fire escape caught the purse neatly in one hand, never hesitating in his pursuit. Dressed in black topped by a sweeping leather duster, moving with purpose and not satisfied with the simple recovery of the stolen purse, he jogged up the noisy metal stairs and leaped onto the roof, landing in a graceful crouch and hesitating only long enough to spot the fleeing thief. Crunching steps on tarry roof gravel traced his pursuit, the duster flapping out behind him as he gained on the creature. Dark hair, pale skin, the hint of a fang . . .

The little demon gave a squeak of fear and re-doubled its scuttling efforts, heading straight for the opposite edge of the roof. "It was only a purse!" it cried back over its shoulder. "Gimme a break here!"

But they both knew that wasn't going to happen. And they knew which of them was faster—he who closed on the demon with such intent, prepared to make sure this particular creature menaced no more of Los Angeles's unsuspecting tourists.

Except the demon reached the edge of the roof a few precious steps before its pursuer, and launched itself out into the darkness—with no strength or speed inherent in its scrabbling flight, but not needing those things. It spread its arms and legs, revealing a flap of skin running from scrawny elbow to knobby knee, and sailed lightly down to the next roof barely one story below.

It wasn't such a big jump, not for a vampire running full speed and full strength. But the black-clad pursuer put on the brakes, stumbling to an abrupt halt that left him teetering at the edge. His coat billowed around him, his silhouette barely visible against the night sky.

On the roof below, the ratty demon cavorted, dancing his victory and flinging all manner of rude gestures at the hero somehow stymied by the narrow space between the buildings and the minor drop between roofs.

The hero turned away from the display. The swirling duster revealed a lanky form not quite at home in the sleek black clothing, not quite as muscular or athletic as the image his clothing conveyed. His dark, spiky-moussed hair had no highlights, a bad dye job here in this city where the inhabitants were finely attuned to such things. And even with the glint of fang at his lip, his forehead remained perfectly human . . . at least, to those who would know the difference.

He resettled his glasses on his nose and went to return the purse.

CHAPTER TWO

Angel's bedroom lay swathed in a false twilight created by drawn curtains. Angel himself lay swathed in twisted bedcovers, restless . . . frowning in his sleep. Marginally aware that something reached into his privacy, touching him. Whispering to him.

Nebulous dreams of uncomfortable passions. Exposed throats, warm pulses, an angry young man once named Liam now made powerful. Touched by those things familiar, Angelus stirs. Caressed by gentle waves of dark power. . . .

Angelus stirs.

Pencil in hand, Cordelia Chase put aside her magazine and leaned over the lobby desk of the abandoned—*mostly* abandoned—Hyperio Hotel that Angel Investigations called headquarters and that Angel himself called home, greeting

7

him as he came down the lobby stairs with his not-an-early-evening-person face on. *Barely twilight and he's up already? Not likely to be cheery.*

Just the time for some distinctly cheery news. "A woman came by. She wanted to thank you again for getting her purse back from some rat-thing."

He lifted a hand in acknowledgment and shuffled past to the fridge behind the front counter, evidently ready for a second serving of breakfast blood. Definitely not all there, with the cuffs of his black jeans dragging below his boot heels and his gray sweater rumpled. Cordelia was willing to bet he hadn't even fastened the snap to his jeans, and she was never wrong about Things Clothes.

Men. They're all alike, even the vampire versions.

After a gulp, he said, "Didn't see any rat-things last night."

"She sure seemed to be full of appreciation." Cordelia retrieved her magazine and filled in one of the five-letter words of the painfully simple crossword puzzle. "Considering that her appreciation came with a check attached and all. I don't understand why she kept muttering about not being able to find the main office, though."

He merely grunted, and she gave him a sharp look. "You're not having trouble sleeping again, are you?"

Except she didn't mean trouble *sleeping*, she

8

meant trouble with dreams, like when Darla had invaded his nights, luring him back toward the Angelus side of his nature and driving a rift between Angel and the gang at Angel Investigations. And maybe he hadn't let Angelus out, not really . . . but Cordelia could still feel the hurt of his inexplicable rejection, and that was bad enough. *So no, I don't really mean trouble* sleeping.

Angel flinched ever so slightly. He, too, remembered. He lowered his cheap plastic tumbler and gave her a look with more thought behind it. Thought, and perhaps a little bit of guilt.

"Not a great expression," she told him bluntly.

He hesitated, then said, "It's just a mood. Isn't a guy entitled to a mood now and then?"

She drummed the pen against the counter and considered him. Yes, a definite hint of guilt. And Angel was a take-charge, do what had to be done, *whatever* had to be done kind of guy. Lots of remorse over things he couldn't change, things he'd done, lots of regret . . . but the guilt? Guilt meant something he was afraid he might *do*. Time to worry. "Nope," she said decisively. "No moods. Not for you."

He looked a little hurt, but Cordelia held firm. There were some luxuries that a guy walking around with a wantonly evil vampire personality lurking beneath his soul just couldn't take. Flirting with darkness . . . that would be one of them.

But then he realized what she'd said a moment earlier and latched on to it with not so subtle relief. "A check? We got money?"

She retrieved it from the computer desk and waved it at him. "Money," she confirmed. "Think paycheck! And I'm going to go right over to her bank and cash it."

He drained the tumbler and left it sitting on the counter. "Cordy . . . the money's not ours. I was *here* last night. No rat-things. The woman's mistaken me for someone else."

She gave him an incredulous look. "And how likely is *that*?"

He shrugged. "How likely is anything that happens in this city?"

She had to admit he had a point there. She looked wistfully at the check. "I suppose I could hold it for a couple of days. . . ."

Wesley Wyndham-Pryce wandered out of his office—once the hotel manager's office, with a huge window between office and lobby and a solemn decor of dusty green and dark wood. He was in his rare rugged look today—a day's worth of seal brown beard, a flannel shirt with rolled sleeves . . . a year ago Cordelia would have bet he didn't *own* a flannel shirt. But the refined features of his face were as serious as ever, as were gray eyes that often seemed to turn dark with the solemn wisdom of someone who knows all the things that can go wrong with the world.

Well, *most* of them. There was always something new and improved going on.

Wesley jammed his spiffy new black lacquered chopsticks into the contents of a Chinese take-out carton with finality as he swallowed a last mouthful.

Angel winced at the stabbing gesture. "Kind of rude, don't you think?"

Unaffected, Wes barely glanced at the utensils. "They're hardly up to the standards set by Buffy's Mr. Pointy. I think you have nothing to fear. Now what's this about money?"

"We have some," Cordelia said, and waved the check again, giving Angel an accusing look. "*He* wants me to give it back, as if anyone could possibly mistake him for somebody else. Plus, he's all moody, which as we know never bodes well."

Angel stood at the end of the counter and said with exasperation, "Cordelia, I'm just—"

The main lobby doors burst open—an event that should have happened with much less frequency. A man ran into the lobby, stumbling over the step as he tried to take in all directions at once. He wore an old rumpled coat over a hound-stooth sweater-vest, and polyester pants that should have been burned a decade earlier, and Cordelia mentally assigned him to the clothes Fashion Police for the day. The man raked a frantic gaze across them, looking and not finding. He

hesitated upon reaching Angel and almost imper-
ceptibly shook his head in rejection.

"I need to find Angel," he blurted.

The young Tuingas demon hadn't waited for the
priests to ponder his punishment; he hadn't even
waited for them to find out about the missing
deathstone. The sneeze, the fall, the physical
touch-chain of his amulet to the deathstone—only
two degrees of separation!—he'd known what had
happened. He'd known he was responsible. And
he'd known what had to be done . . . and what
would happen to Los Angeles if he didn't do it.

He took it upon himself to leave the peaceful
pocket dimension where his particular branch of
the Tuingas clan spent most of their time, and he
entered the human world to find the deathstone.

Tracking the stone hadn't been hard at all. Their
pocket dimension was anchored in Los Angeles;
anyone or thing emerging from it generally found
themselves in one of the unfathomable concrete
river channels veining the city. This fact combined
with the seasonal floods made the Tuingas clan
very much a set of look-before-you-leap demons.

Look-before-you-leap wasn't a luxury that the
young Tuingas had had. So he'd leaped, and he'd
landed on hard concrete, and he'd followed the
stone's distinctive emanations, knowing he had
very little time.

He might not be a priest, but he was in the shrines on a daily basis. He'd learned well enough what would happen should an exposed stone not be recovered. Removed from its protective shrine and its protective pocket dimension, the stone's emissions—normally experienced only by pre-pared visitors under priestly supervision—would flood this city's demons with the very impression left on the deathstone. In this case, by a warrior, fighting at peak emotion for a just cause. A warrior who'd left impressions of his death fury, his intent to avenge the cause . . . all the passions and moti-vations of a warrior in his last fight . . . moments before it became his last fight.

Oh, why this *one?* the young demon moaned to himself. This potent new stone, so strong that it had tasteful warning signs inscribed upon its pedestal. So potent that no unprotected demon would be able to resist the wave after wave of emotion it emitted. And the deathstone itself—activated by the warrior's death, kept in the shrine for its own purity and protection—would be just as sensitive to the resulting mood of the city.

The young Tuingas didn't even want to think about that. He wanted to be gone from here long before the feedback became strong enough to ex-press itself in the city. And so he'd been heartened to track the stone as easily as he had, from the one who'd found it and the next day put it in a suburban garage sale as a unique garden stone, to the one who'd bought it for a paltry sum, having no notion of the pricelessness of the deathstone but just savvy enough to think that his friend, a collector of odd artifacts, might be interested in it.

For an equally paltry sum and with a determinedly casual expression, that friend had indeed acquired the stone. With just as much determination but no opportunity, the Tuingas lurked and waited and stalked and . . .

Waited.

And the collector had known. The young Tuingas could see by his actions, how he carefully and quickly packed the stone up in its odd, oversized bag. But the man's admiration for the stone had nothing to do with its intangible value to the Tuingas . . . the lingering presence of a hero and loved one. There was no respect in his face. There was only greed. To judge by the man's other such transactions, he would keep the stone only long enough to find a wealthy buyer, either not knowing or not caring about the consequences. Or figuring, as many humans seem to, that somehow he would be the exception to the rule.

The young Tuingas grew frustrated. Limited to hiding in shadows and waiting for opportunity, he followed the man to a temporary cluster of dwellings . . . and there he ran into *real* trouble. Where the unfamiliar nature of L.A. had not deterred him, where his lack of sophistication had not discouraged him, the man's wise precautions—including no doubt a newly minted amulet of his own—stopped the Tuingas short.

The young demon couldn't enter the building. Not from the roof or the windows or the so obvious door. He tried and he tried again, and found himself inexorably repelled. The man had visitors . . . people bearing food and messages and then another man, younger, all dressed in black and awkwardly keeping to shadows. But for the Tuingas there was no entry, so he waited. He watched. He wondered what the priests had said when they found his crudely scrawled note of intent to reclaim the deathstone, and he wondered what would happen to him when he finally returned. He'd already lost weight. His long-nose hung limp and unhappy.

But eventually the man had emerged.

The young Tuingas had followed him.

"I need to find Angel," the man blurted.

He's crazy, Cordelia decided at once, and applied her politely-interested-but-really-not face for him.

"I know I'm not supposed to come here, that he likes to keep his street people under cover. But he's not at the main office address he gave me and *I need to see him*—"

"Calm yourself," Wesley said, glancing at Angel

with wry bemusement as he set aside his take-out carton. "We'll try to help you, but—"

Angel looked at the man who had so decisively and unexpectedly dismissed him, and then down at himself. He straightened his sweater, surreptitiously tugging his jeans up to fasten the snap.

I knew it. But Cordelia savored the private triumph only for an instant. She gestured at Angel. "But this *is* Ange—"

The man waved a hand in vehement denial. A bowling bag weighed the other hand down, a battered old thing with handles that barely seemed to be attached. It seemed heavy in his hand, but its slack sides looked empty. "I know all about the look-alike he sends out on the street to confuse those who might be following him," he said. "Don't try that charade on me. I need the *real* Angel, and I need him—"

The doors crashed open. Really crashed, as in right off the hinges. Even Angel blinked at that, and at the distinctly inhuman creature that bounded through them, heading straight for the desperate man and his bowling ball.

"—right *now!*" cried the man, his voice raising an octave. Maybe two.

"I'll fake it," Angel muttered, and put himself between man and demon as the man dove for one of the lobby columns, clinging to it from behind.

The creature hesitated, long enough to offer a brief impression of alligator skin, a flexible fifth appendage swung neatly over its shoulder, and beady black eyes focused entirely on his prey.

"Hey," Angel said, annoyed. "I'm right here in front of you. And I gotta tell you, it bothers me when demons forget to knock."

It saw him then. It reached for him with every apparent intent of tossing him aside, and Angel responded with every apparent intent of holding ground. The demon used its weight to shove Angel back and back again, up against the column behind which the man quivered—and not so incidentally beside which Cordelia had been standing. It pushed Angel right off his feet—and up—to dangle against the column.

Cordelia's anger flared. Was that any way to behave in someone else's hotel? She hauled back and kicked the demon. She kicked it in the shin—or what she thought was a shin—she kicked it in the thigh—ditto—and she kicked it in the groin—*definitely not sure about that one*. It didn't appear to notice, and, panting, she staggered back to reconsider.

At the far lobby wall, Wesley flung open the glass-front door to the weapons cabinet and grabbed something sharp at random; he tossed it to Cordelia. She made no attempt to catch it—not until it clattered to the floor and she could identify the not-sharp parts of the short curving sword. Then she scooped it up and slapped it into Angel's open hand. *Just like a scrub nurse,* she thought. *Perfect for a guest role on* E.R. *That is, if they could lure George Clooney back.*

In one smooth motion, Angel swept the blade deeply across the demon's midsection. The demon instantly dropped him, and before Angel could get back to his feet or Cordelia could catch her breath or Wesley could arrive with his own weapon of choice, the thing let out a garbled wail of agonized defeat and collapsed in upon itself.

And continued to collapse in on itself, so by the time they gathered to stand in a circle around it, there was little left but a mound of faintly hissing goo. As they watched, it bubbled slightly and settled even further.

"May I just say," Cordelia began, waving her hand under her nose in a futile attempt to dispel the smell of the thing, "ew."

"Ew," Angel agreed, and looked at Wesley, who gave the slightest of shrugs.

"Ew," he said, but of course he had to add, "indeed," just so he could sound like his usual scholarly, stiff-upper-lipped self.

Gunn entered through the broken lobby door wearing his nothing-surprises-me-anymore expression, which totally went with the shaved head and the blocky, oversized shirt that hid too much of what Cordelia had always considered very nice shoulders, not to mention jeans that could have been tighter for her taste. He'd given up on the skullcap bandanna lately . . . probably couldn't keep it from turning his underwear pink in the laundry. He walked in backward to assess the damage from the inside, brow raised. He turned around as he reached their little circle, his feet just out of the danger zone. "Whoa," he said, wrinkling his nose in offense. "Not your mother's perfume."

"No," Cordelia said grimly. Typical day so far—moody Angel, inexplicable identity crisis, and dissolving demons. "Not your mother's pile of goo, either. I mean, how *rude*. It's not going to be easy to identify *that*."

"Best make a sketch while it's still fresh in your mind," Wesley suggested.

"Also not an image I want to contemplate," Cordelia told him, but went to grab the notebook they kept for such things—mostly so she could sketch things from her visions. Goo Demon apparently wasn't vision-worthy.

Angel turned to the man with the bowling ball, who looked as if he hoped they'd forgotten about him. "We need to talk."

As Cordelia slapped her notebook on the counter and started to sketch, thinking wistfully of all those high school art classes she'd skipped, the man eased around the edge of the room. And as Cordelia decided there probably hadn't been anything in those classes that would apply to drawing demons, anyway, the man edged toward the broken door and escape.

"Talking." Angel's gaze followed the man's retreat. "As in answering questions. We have plenty of questions to choose from."

"Identikit," Cordelia murmured, sketching away. Erasing. Erasing more. "A demon Identikit. That's what we need."

"I do have a new guide," Wesley said, with deceptive lack of reaction to the slyly outward-bound visitor. "Fairly recent, and it uses the same basic identification template as the *Newcomb's Wildflower Guide*. I'll see if I can dig it up."

Their escaping client was so close to the door that he probably thought he had it made. But more smoothly, more quickly than the man could possibly anticipate, Angel stepped in front of him. Inches away, as though he'd been there all along and simply *appeared*. "That's not talking, that's *leaving*."

Ordinary words, but there was something in his voice that made Cordelia look up from her work, startled. Angel loomed over the man, and she would have said he was all but fang-face.

"The fight's over, Angel," Wesley said, a note of

worry in his voice that made Cordelia think he'd seen the same thing.

Or maybe the fight *wasn't* over. For yet another figure burst through the abused lobby doors— except this one had apparently been shopping in Angel's closet. Of the same height only gawkier, his hair darkened by a bad home dye job, his glasses slightly askew, his human face a caricature of dismay, his entire appearance a caricature of Angel. In one swift look he took in the scene before him.

There was a thick moment of silence.

Then he muttered what could only have been an extremely bad word, turned on his heel, and burst right back out the doors and into the night.

The fellow with the bowling ball cried, "No! Wait!" and dodged around Angel, breaking into a run as he called out after the most recent arrival-departure. "Angel, wait! We have to talk!"

"Yes, indeed," Angel muttered to himself, his face full of grim. "That's just exactly what we're going to do." And out the door he went, snatching his duster from a chair on the way.

Cordelia reached for the check from the rat-thing woman and flicked it thoughtfully against her fingers. "This is starting to make a little more sense." *Mistaken identity, Angel sorta-look-alike . . .*

"Do you think so?" Wesley asked. "Because, frankly, I don't think it makes any sense at all."

21

"Don't look at *me*," Gunn said. "All I know about is this pile of stinky goo here."

"Whose day is it?" Wesley said, but there was resignation in his voice. As there well might be—even if it had been Cordelia's day to catch the lobby messes, she wasn't about to get any closer to this one. Besides, she had sketches to make.

"I know darn sure it's not the guy who didn't *make* the mess," Gunn said. "Besides, I've got places to be."

"Perhaps," Wesley said with exaggerated weariness, "you might be so good as to see if there's anything you can do with the door. Just to hold it for tonight. Not," he added dryly, "that it seems to have been any good at keeping people out in the first place."

"Or *in*," Cordelia murmured, looking at the doors as if she could see right through the remains to whatever Angel had encountered when he caught up with the man, the bowling ball bag, and the poor imitation of Angel himself. "I wonder if we'll ever know what that was all about."

Wesley headed for the cleaning supplies, grimly rolling his sleeves even higher. "I suspect it'll go down as an inexplicable moment. Those do have their charm, after all. The demon's dead, the potential client has run away . . . the world was never in danger."

Cordelia frowned at him. *How much more could you possibly tempt the Fates than by suggesting the world was safe?*

Gunn gave a wise shake of his head. "Bowling night. Worse than a full moon."

Angel should have been able to catch up with them. He should have been able to catch up with them, do barrel rolls around them, and cut them off short, all while wearing a smile.

If he'd been paying attention.

He eased to a halt in the middle of an alley, feeling more than a little foolish. He hadn't the foggiest idea when they'd zigged and he hadn't. By now they'd probably zagged as well and weren't anywhere to be found.

Because he *hadn't* been paying attention. He'd been caught up in an unexpected anger, pouring it into the speed and effort of the run until the run became the point and not the chase.

He stood in the middle of the alley and looked at his hands—they trembled—and then ran fingers over his face, confirming what he already knew. Fang-face, right out here in public. He took a breath—or what would have been a breath, if he'd actually needed to breathe—and felt the gruesome features ease back into normal flesh. What was *that* about? Temper over a bad vampire wanna-be? An *Angel* wanna-be?

He didn't think so. He recalled the dark thoughts that had haunted his sleep and then clung to him beyond waking, and he thought there was more to his reaction . . . even as he hoped that there *wasn't*. But now . . . he was on his guard. He wouldn't let this happen again.

Especially not where the gang could see.

He looked at his hands again—the trembling had stopped—and then jammed them in his duster pockets. He didn't feel like facing them right now, and he *really* didn't feel like explaining how he'd lost his quarry. On the other hand . . .

On the other hand, they needed him to prove he was dependable right now. That he wasn't going to—*again*—run off and do his own thing, shutting them out. Hurting them. The memory of Cordelia's pained expression as he'd helped her off the dead client's kitchen floor and asked if she was all right, the uncharacteristically unforgiving tone of her voice as she'd said, "You hurt my feelings." He didn't ever want to face that again.

So he stared down the dark alley a moment longer, exchanged a long glance with a wise-looking cat, and headed back for the hotel. Being dependable. Responsible.

Faking it.

Angel entered through the courtyard doors, avoiding Gunn at work on the front entrance. Inside, Cordelia sat straight-backed at the computer, entering search words into their fast-growing demon database. She didn't look happy. Without looking away from the screen, she spoke to the lobby at large and said, "This is getting me nowhere. It can't find a fifth appendage unless I can give it a name, and I have no *idea* what that thing was. I'm not even sure I *want* to know. And what did it want with that man, anyway? It followed him right *here,* like a tracking dog or something."

Wesley's voice came from the lobby, down near the floor. Somewhere behind the round booth unit where the demon had finally gone down. "Unless Angel comes back with answers, that demon is our only lead."

"I could get a vision," Cordelia said, half with a wince and half with hope. The visions exacted a worrisome toll. A rising toll.

"The demon's our only lead," Angel said flatly, announcing himself in the process.

"Oh?" Wesley stood, surprised by Angel's presence—or perhaps just surprised that he'd returned alone. Wesley held a black garbage bag as far away from himself as he could.

It looked full.

In his other hand—a latex-gloved hand, one of the elbow-length gloves available through large animal veterinary supply companies—he held an odd, large lump of something. An actual clue? Or just leftover demon. . . .

"What's that?" Angel said, nodding at the lump as he moved deeper into the lobby.

Wesley glanced at it. "Part of *this*," he said, hefting the bag slightly. "I thought I might take a closer look." On the floor beside the roundchair was a gallon of Nature's Miracle—Stain and Odor Remover for Pet Accidents! Wesley gave it a skeptical expression. "After another healthy dose of cleanser."

Gunn left the partially secured doors to look down into the lobby—to look at Angel, specifically. "No luck?"

Angel gave the slightest of shrugs, but knew it wouldn't be that easy.

"Hey, the way you charged out of here, I figured you'd bring 'em back with tread marks." Gunn hefted the hammer he held, obviously imagining what he might have done with it. "I mean, hey— with that you-looking guy on hand, your mirror problem would be solved, right?"

"I charged one way, they charged another," Angel said simply.

"Huh," Cordelia said, sounding very much like she suspected there was more to it.

There was, of course. The anger that nudged at him even now. Anger he couldn't give in to . . . couldn't even reveal hints of. But he could give her a dark look; she was used to that.

"Don't be a poor loser," she said smartly—but as he'd hoped, he'd distracted her. Banter was safe ground, and if her eyes—luxuriously tilted dark eyes set above strong cheekbones—lingered on him as if she might see something revealing, soon enough she returned to her work. She made a face at the computer monitor and said, "This is a waste of time, guys. Wesley, where's that book you were talking about?"

"Hold on," he said, and walked off with his nastiness-in-a-bag, taking the shortest route to the alley and their garbage bin. He came back with a bowl, put the lump of something in it, and splashed the stain and odor remover over the top of it. Generously.

"Nice conversation piece," Cordelia said when he put it on the lobby counter. "Ugh, not there. It stinks!"

"It should be better shortly," he said. "Just let me wash my hands."

"You're wearing gloves," she pointed out.

"Humor me," he told her, and disappeared into the hotel counter staff bathroom. When he came back out he was drying his hands. "I believe I know how Lady Macbeth must have felt," he said, and tossed the towel over his shoulder to duck into his office. "Here we are," he said upon reemerging. He held out a book, and Cordelia left her desk to reach for it, casting a wary eye on the Lump of Something on her way by.

"It looks like a stone," she said. "But it's a really ugly stone."

"As stones go," Gunn said, and smirked.

Both Wesley and Angel cast him frowns, and Gunn shrugged. "I'm a guy," he said. "So sue me. Anyway, it's not like we have anything to work with here. Maybe Wes is right and it's not worth the trouble."

Wesley protested, "I don't recall saying—"

"Inexplicable moment," Gunn said, unmoved. *"The world was never in any danger.* In case you ever doubted my memory."

A little gathering of his brow gave away Wesley's reluctance to actually take such a thing as safety for granted. "All the same—"

Cordelia ignored them all, flipping through the demon book with dismay. "Look at this!" she said, a big frown on a mouth that was really meant for smiling. "I don't even know where to start."

"It's quite simple." Wesley flipped it open to the beginning pages. "It's just like a flower guide, or a tree guide. You started with the broadest level of characteristics—for instance, does it go on all fours or stand upright—and narrow it down. How many limbs, how many eyes . . . see this category, for instance. *Two symmetrical limbs* or *three whorled limbs*—"

"Four bi-symmetrical limbs and a waving thing," Cordelia said with certainty. "It's that waving thing that keeps tripping me up. Maybe I should get Fred in on this. She's good at this sort of thing. Books, I mean." *If she ever feels safe enough to*

28

come down. Cordelia heaved a great dramatic sigh and took the book. "Okay, I'll keep trying. You know, just in case it's actually the end of the world. Again."

A troubled look crossed Wesley's face; he squinched his nose ever so slightly. "I think I'll just wash my hands once more."

And suddenly Angel couldn't deal with the whole postattack scene, all this casual normality. Not with his anger buzzing around inside his head like a saw, echoing off itself to create a reverberation that kept building and building and—

"I'm outta here," he said.

"Oh, good," Wesley said, entirely clueless. "See if you can track those two down."

Angel didn't bother to correct him. Let them think he was out hunting their interlopers, finding the Angel impersonator—the sudden image of a Las Vegas full of Angel impersonators nearly did him in right then and there—when he was really simply not being *there*. At his own hotel. In the middle of his human friends, trying to hide his vampire feelings.

He went to Caritas.

"We were too late," the elder priest intoned in a voice of doom that vibrated audibly in his long nose. "The young one is dead, and now we're missing *two* deathstones."

Six under-priests huddled around the empty pedestal, resplendent in their broad sash-belts but reserved and tense in posture. One of them said, "The young one's deathstone is entirely raw. It must be recovered at once."

"This may not be as difficult as feared," the elder said. "While the warrior's stone is in the hands of one who hopes to gain from it, I have reports that the young one's stone resides with those who lack all understanding of its true nature. It will not be as well-protected."

Another under-priest tugged nervously at his sash and said, "What of the families? Do they know anything yet?"

The elder priest shook his head—a broad gesture indeed on a creature with a neck so thick. "All are under the impression that we're remodeling this area in honor of the new stone. The young one is assumed to be involved. But we cannot keep up this deception for long."

"Not when you consider the consequences of the warrior's stone going unprotected in the middle of that tightly packed city," said the first under-priest. He was a strong individual, and he stood quietly—not fiddling with his sash or tugging the tops of his stubby round ears or even cracking his toes. "I judge we have very little time. I would like to volunteer to go to the city. I have some familiarity with it. I'll bring back the young one's stone."

"That must be first priority," the elder agreed. "Both because of the stone's raw condition and the likelihood of quick success. I intend for another of you to keep track of the warrior's stone in the meantime. When you"—and he nodded at the first under-priest—"have returned with the raw stone, you will go back out to work together to retrieve the warrior's stone."

The under-priests politely clicked their teeth together in acquiescence.

But none of them thought it would be quite that simple. And all of them knew the trouble was already starting.

CHAPTER THREE

It might be pig's blood, but it was fresh and warm and served with a mint leaf up against the inside of the glass. Angel leaned over the bar and took a contemplative sip. Smooth and salty and just the right amount of tang. Just what Angel needed to take the edge off his nerves after the way the evening had started.

"Good vintage," he told Lorne, who was busy serving up something totally disgusting to a Veroscini demon several seats away. Angel thought he saw something move in the thick mustard-colored liquid. On stage, a barrel-chested demon in a leather vest and chain-mail breeches bellowed "Bat out of Hell" in nothing even approaching Meatloaf's original rendition.

"Nothing but corn-fed pigs for *this* bar," Lorne said, appearing to take no notice of the Veroscini's misbehaving drink. He exchanged a few quick words with the scaly demon and came back toward Angel counting a handful of coins. "No tip from *him* tonight," Lorne muttered, smoothing his dark orange tie. "Just one of those nights."

"How's that?" Angel asked him, taking another sip and letting it warm further in his mouth before swallowing. Beside him, a tree frog–like creature clambered up the bar stool, elbowing Angel along the way. Slith demon. Angel didn't scowl, not quite.

"Service!" the little demon demanded in his little demon voice, sitting on the stool with his twiggy arms and legs akimbo. "I want one of your Banana Slugs!"

"Banana Slug?" Angel asked as Lorne rolled his eyes—so expressive against that green skin of his—and reached under the bar for the small refrigerator built into it. "New drink? I don't remember that one being on the menu—"

Lorne slapped a cocktail napkin down on the bar. On top of it was a giant slug—fresh chilled, still feebly writhing.

"Oh," Angel said. "Of course. Banana Slug. Right."

"Where's the cinnamon?" the demon demanded, standing up on the bar stool to plant his splayed hands on the bar and glare first at the slug, then at Lorne.

"Yeah, yeah," Lorne said, and produced a salt shaker filled with cinnamon. He gave an expert flick of the wrist, powdering the glistening slug, and turned back to Angel as if they'd never been interrupted. *"That's* why no tip. They're all like that tonight. There's some nasty mojo on the streets tonight—don't tell me you don't feel it. Slith demons like this one, for instance. Normally as mild as you'd please."

"No kidding," Angel said, sorry he'd asked. And trying hard not to sound too interested as he sensed Lorne winding up for the long answer on top of the short. He should have just kept his own mouth shut.

Or maybe that was just the nasty mojo talking.

"Do you have any idea how hard it is to maintain my own cheerfully friendly demeanor when those all around me have given in to the Dark Side of the Force?" Lorne continued, gesturing at the stage. "Even with my amazingly perceptive self-aware-ness, some things are hard to take." Another demon had grabbed the mike, dressed in oversized denims and a hooded sweatshirt with the hood drawn up and tied. He started in on a rap song, but between the lisp and the interference of his tusks, couldn't begin to keep up with the rhythm. He quickly fell to mumbling and grunting—at least until he ran into a foul word, which he gleefully shouted with perfect enunciation. Lorne *tsked* and shook his head. "Now that young woman needs the influence of the elders she's flaunting right now."

"Young woma—," Angel started, but didn't go

any further. He well remembered meeting Lorne's severely undoting and not to mention masculine-ish mother in Pylea.

Perhaps it hadn't been a good idea to come here, good blood or no. He'd needed to get his head together, and somehow Caritas had pulled together all its most distracting denizens to keep him from doing just that. He stood, digging into his pocket for change—but when he glanced up, he found Lorne giving him a pensive look. "What?"

"Hum something for me, *babushka*."

Angel shot him an annoyed look, but experience had taught him Lorne was nothing if not persistent. He hunted for a song, desperate to avoid "Bat out of Hell"—now running endlessly through his mind—for too many reasons to number. Finally he just made a flat-sounding, *"Humhumhum."*

Lorne gave a satisfied nod. "As I thought. You're in a bad place, my friend."

No news to Angel.

Lorne added, "And for no reason that I can see."

That came as news. Lorne could always pinpoint those tricky, slippery motivations that people tried to hide—even from themselves. Angel suddenly realized he'd been harboring a well-hidden hope that Lorne would offer him some easy answer, a concrete problem upon which to blame his inadvertent fang-face, his distraction, even the day's dreams.

Things he couldn't blame on the irritating presence of an imposter about whom he'd only just learned. "What do you mean, for no reason?"

"Are my words not coming out in English? What I said, sweetcheeks. *No reason I can see.* You've got the mood, all right, but there's nothing particularly driving behind it. Unless you can enlighten me?" He gave the surly crowd a meaningful glance.

"Haw!" little demon guffawed in mid-chew, spraying Angel with bits of slug. His attention was on the stage, where the excessively baggy pants on the rapping demon had contrived to fall down and bare far too much gnarled flesh.

"That doesn't mean you don't need to be careful," Lorne said, ignoring the interruption. "*Au contraire*, I think you need to be more careful than ever. Until you find the source of your disquiet, you never know when—Angel, are you listening?"

Angel had, in fact, been swiping slug bits off his duster. "I hear you. In fact, I think the best thing to do is find a nice quiet room in the hotel and—" He paused, suddenly aware of the Slith demon's intent regard.

"Angel," the demon said, swallowing what was left of his mouthful.

At least he'd *swallowed*.

"You're not Angel! I know Angel! I've had drinks with Angel! Angel is my friend—and you're not Angel!"

Angel glanced at Lorne, brow raised. "You know this guy?"

"He's been here a couple times before," Lorne said. "But I'm not the only demon hangout in L.A. If he's been palling around with someone he calls Angel, it wasn't in here."

"All right," Angel said to the Slith. "Angel is your friend. Let's talk about Angel. Like where I can get hold of him."

The Slith stood back up on his stool, looking up at Angel with his hands jammed defiantly on his nearly nonexistent hips. "You don't get hold of Angel," he said. "He gets hold of *you!*" And he took a prodigious leap into the seating area, bouncing off several tables until he reached the door.

"See?" Lorne said, looking sadly at the empty plate and its generous sprinkling of cinnamon and slug slime. "No tip."

Gunn had places to be, all right. Fresh-air places, at least compared with the Hyperion's current *eau de demon*. He looked at the teens gathered around the pavilion at MacArthur Park. Sullen. That stood to reason . . . they'd come off the streets to meet him here, for a single evening leaving behind the bleak rebellion that made up their lives to consider another way.

Sullen, but they were *here*. And that said a lot too.

Sinthea and Tyree would be the tough ones. Their expressions said as much, and their body language . . . he'd seen them around. For them he'd need to find responsibilities . . . and just the right amount of toughness back at them. The others . . . they'd present their own problems, but mostly they'd follow along with the other two. Fifteen of them, and he thought maybe half would stick with it.

"We're here to start neighborhood watch training," he said. "You come for any other reason? Time to leave."

Sinthea pushed back sleek black hair, courtesy of her Asian blood. Her deep brown skin came from somewhere else altogether, and the streets gave her her attitude. She said, "I heard this was better than *neighborhood watch* training. Special. It'll give us an edge." She gave him a hard look, waiting for him to confirm it.

"Could be," he said. "Probably not what you're thinking, though."

Tyree—as tall as Gunn, deepest blue-black skin and hair just shy of shaved entirely, gave Gunn a look of disgust. "Quit playing us. You think we're stupid? This ain't no *official* neighborhood watch program."

Gunn smiled happily, which took them by surprise. "No," he said. "It's not." He gave them a moment to think about it. "Look—you all know the streets, right? You *live* the streets."

There was a general murmur of agreement, some fist-bumping, plenty of posturing.

"Then you've seen things you haven't mentioned to anyone else. You know things go on that most people won't admit. You know it's not just drugs and gangs and dirty cops that we have to worry about."

Some of them nodded; most of them looked uncertainly to Tyree and Sinthea. Finally Sinthea gave a short, defiant nod. "We know."

Gunn said, "We can do something about it. But first you've gotta understand what you're up against. You've gotta know how to fight it. You don't waste yourself thinking that *tough* is good enough to do the job. You've got to use teamwork and you've got to use your brains."

The youngest teen there, a wiry Latino who looked strong and fast for his age, said, "And why should we? We don't got enough to worry about?"

"Yeah, it's a tough world," Gunn said without sympathy. "And I'm sure you're all busy being cool in it, and that great big load of righteous mad you're carrying around probably tires you out." He spotted a group of three murmuring among themselves, drifting off toward the small copse of trees between the pavilion and Wilshire Boulevard . . . minor drug deal, going down on the spot. He ignored it. "Here's the deal. There're things in this city to make you crazy—the people going hungry, the people getting killed, the people disrespecting you and looking down at you and acting like they know what's best for you." The words hit home; he could see the mood change, the resentment coming closer to the surface. "The thing about anger is . . . it can use *you* or you can use *it*. Personally, I like using *it*. And I like doing it in a way that no one else knows how. I like making the difference that no one else can make."

"Yeah, but do we get to fight?" the Latino asked. "Or is this one of those nicey-nice games you want us to play?"

Gunn just smiled. Big.

"Welcome back," Cordelia said as she spotted Angel trying to slink through the lobby unseen. A token effort . . . if he wanted to go unseen, he would. Simple as that. "No customers, no visions. Which you know already, since we didn't call you with any hot tips or anything. Oh, wait—in order to get a call, your cell phone's got to be *on*, doesn't it?"

He got a quietly desperate look on his face, obviously wishing he *had* come through the lobby in stealth mode. Cordelia flipped through her latest copy of *Entertainment Weekly*, unaffected. The lobby was clean(ish), the vision factor was at zero, and she was about to call it quits for the night. She could afford to be serene.

"Batteries," he said. "I swear, I charged them—"

"Uh-huh." She tore her attention away from an article about Harrison Ford. "Look, you might as well talk. There's obviously something bothering you." And as usual, he'd rather be Broody Guy than get it off his chest. She bet he never even screamed into his pillow. Maybe they needed one of those squishy head things some people had around the office to poke and squeeze for stress release.

Except she supposed they *did* often have squishy head things around the office. And they usually got rid of them just as fast as humanly— vampirely—possible.

"Talk?" Angel said, inching a step closer to the stairs. Mr. Big Scary Vampire, about to run from a little conversation.

"Yes, *talk*. If you plan to get all broody and moody and start keeping to yourself again, you should know that our old office space is still for rent." Office as in she and Gunn and Wesley, out on their own and doing just fine. Except for Wes getting shot, of course. And Cordelia herself acquiring a third eye in the back of her head. *But aside from that*—

"Is there a problem?" Wesley emerged from the bathroom, where he'd been washing his hands again. Not that Cordelia could blame him. Dissolving demon stink clung to the lobby like . . . like . . .

On the other hand, there *was* nothing like dissolving demon stink.

"No problem," Angel said, just a little too quickly. "Any luck identifying that demon?"

Cordelia sighed, trading the magazine for the demon guide; she'd marked her place with one of Wesley's new chopsticks, much to his annoyance. "This wasn't any more help than the database. Not yet, anyway. We're still looking." She gave her magazine a guilty glance. "I mean, we *will* be. But it's late, you know?" A glance at her watch confirmed that much. Time for good little demon hunters to be home and abed. Gunn had escaped an hour ago, though she didn't exactly think he'd been headed for bed. There was no telling what Gunn was up to when he wasn't here; she hadn't quite decided if he hunted vampire nests on the side, or if Angel Investigations was actually the side work. "We've been dealing with this all evening, while you were off . . . being off. I gotta think that if it was a big deal, I'd have had a vision about it already."

"Maybe someone else is meant to take care of it," Wesley agreed. "Our interesting and familiar-looking friend from earlier in the evening, perhaps." A faintly disturbed look crossed his face; he lifted his arm and took a sniff of the cotton button-down shirt he wore. "It's not my hands . . . it's *me*."

"I told you," Cordelia said. "It's gonna take a warehouse full of Febreze to get this place back to its old musty self."

Angel probably thought himself off the hook; he turned for the stairs. No way she was gonna give him that—nor Wesley, apparently, for he said, "Any luck on your end?"

"Any luck . . . ?" Angel repeated.

"Finding the two humans who came along with our dearly dissolved demon friend," Wesley said.

Angel hesitated, then said carefully, "I found someone else who's seen the one who . . . looked kinda like . . . ," and he stalled out, looking terribly awkward.

"You," Cordelia filled in, blunt where he was reluctant. "And boy, doesn't he have some nerve. *I'm* the one attached to the Powers That Be with these headaches and visions, and he thinks all he's got to do is look like you—"

"What *is* that all about?" he asked, moving back into the desk area, suddenly more animated. "Guy dresses like me, takes on clients in my name . . ."

"Obviously a desperate man," Wesley said.

Angel sent him an annoyed glance, but it was brief. "He's even been in demon hangouts, making nice. Telling them he's me."

"Plenty of vampire wanna-bes out there," Wesley said. "They generally run in different circles than the real thing, though."

"This isn't a vampire wanna-be," Angel said, and gave himself a rather violent poke in the chest. "This is a *me* wanna-be."

"Look, it's no big deal," Cordelia told him. "It's an admiration thing, you know? For some reason this guy thinks you're hot stuff and that your life is so much better than whatever pathetic excuse for a life he's got on his own. Beats me why he chose you, but there you are."

Ah, she'd gotten his attention. And his most wounded expression. Actually a good sign . . . if he were truly broody he'd just have snarled something and gone upstairs no matter her precious words of wisdom. Cordelia flipped a page of her magazine. More Harrison Ford. Getting a little older now, but she still remembered the first time she'd seen him as Han Solo.

"Hey," Angel said, using his wounded voice to go along with the expression. "I just might have a few good qualities. I mean, maybe not once . . . okay, once I was pretty much a monster. I mean, for a long time I was pretty much a monster. But things have changed now, and I—"

"Harrison Ford," Cordelia said, stabbing her finger at the magazine. "The man saves little kids. In his own helicopter! Now there's something to admire. Money, big toys, and a real hero to boot—"

"Perhaps it was the cost of the helicopter," Wesley suggested, very solemn . . . and entirely not. "This faux Angel had to go for something in his cost range. A few items of black clothing, some hair dye—"

"*Cheap* hair dye," Cordelia added.

"This is *serious*," Angel said. "There's some guy going around reeling in clients with my name. With *our* name. And those clients are expecting real help. Do you think that scrawny wanna-be could have protected that man tonight? Killed that demon?"

Wesley admitted, "I'm not even sure he could have cleaned up after that demon." When Cordelia looked at him, one eyebrow arched in just that way she'd been practicing in the mirror for her skeptical actress look, he said, "Angel has a point, Cordelia. We do have a certain reputation for getting the job done. Even now, that man—"

"And his bowling ball," she said. "What's up with the bowling ball, anyway? A new fetish?"

"—even now, he could be in danger," Wesley continued, undeterred. "Until we figure out which demon came after him, we won't know."

"Right," Angel said. "So we've got to stop this wanna-be. He's a menace. And he's annoying."

"Would that be because he's so much like you?" Cordelia asked.

Wesley said, "First we need to find his client. He's the one in the most danger."

"I don't know about that," Angel said under his breath. But his expression was almost puzzled, as if he struggled with his own reaction.

"I'll tell you what I *do* know," Cordelia said, grabbing her purse from the shelf behind the lobby counter. "First, I get to go home and sleep. Phantom Dennis will worry if it gets much later, and you don't want to know what it's like to live with a ghost on the edge."

"No," Wesley said, a little bemused. "I don't suppose we do."

"Anyway, like I said—no visions. Can't be all that big a deal. We'll look through these books again tomorrow." She looked at Angel, giving him about one zillionth of a second to make objections. "That's that, then!" she said brightly, slinging the satchel-like purse over her shoulder—not her actress-image purse, this one; this was the stake-holding, holy water–stashing version—and heading for the lobby doors. Gunn had managed to nail one of them shut, but the other was too warped and would never close. Home Depot time. Again.

Behind her, she heard Wesley say, "I'm afraid I need to get some rest as well. The books are here, if you want to keep looking."

"I'll be looking, all right," Angel said darkly. "But it won't be in books."

As far as Cordelia could tell, he'd left through the courtyard exit before she even closed the damaged door—at least, as far as it would go—behind her.

• • •

Angel walked the streets, hunting trouble as much as he hunted anything—and even he knew it was probably a good thing that those streets stayed silent and dark before him, almost as if his mood had pushed everything out of the way.

Or maybe as if everyone else had found a dark corner in which to nurse their own inner grumbles.

The fake Angel . . . imitation as admiration? Perhaps to a point. But what this baffling faux Angel had done went beyond. It wasn't imitation, it was assumption of identity. And if you were going to assume an identity, why take that of someone who's trying to atone for several hundred years of heinous behavior? Who would explode into fire when exposed to the sun? Who had the choice of living off people or rats . . . or giving up the hot rush of life for prepackaged pig's blood?

He not only didn't get it, he didn't want anything to do with it. Nor did he want anything to do with the way it stirred up his guilt of those extended years before the Powers That Be had stepped in. Before he'd met Whistler, and . . .

Buffy.

He didn't want to think about those things at all, but something kept dragging his mind back to the anger that had started the whole thought cycle in the first place, and repeatedly started it all over again. So he walked the streets looking for something to distract him and he got into a minor scrap with a demon halfling that didn't even bloody his knuckles and then another, bulldozing through the night. But the anger continued unimpeded, undistracted, and the rest of the world stepped widely around him.

Eventually he returned to the Hyperion none the wiser, wrapped a bungee cord around the handles of the hotel's front doors as a makeshift lock, and wearily climbed the stairs to his own room as dawn broke over the city. The bungee would never stop a determined interloper, but it would slow one down. And they'd do it with enough noise to reach Angel's more than sensitive ears.

Or so he hoped.

It was almost morning by the time he shrugged off his clothes and left them in a manly heap on the floor. Sleep was what he wanted—that thing his body hardly needed but his human mind still craved as much as anything. Deep, quieting sleep.

The Tuingas priest named Khundarr moved uneasily through the streets of the human city, his broad, flat feet slapping barefoot against the concrete with no notice of the broken glass. He was glad for the night . . . and at the same time wary of it. As late as it was, he didn't walk these streets alone—but as a Tuingas priest, he was the only one immune to the deathstone emissions pulsing through the night. The only one truly sane.

Already he could feel the uneasy roil resulting from the demon warrior stone's rising feedback loop—and he could have found his way to the raw new deathstone with his eyes covered and both noses plugged. It reeked of fear and desperation and anger, a shriller note overtop the deep emissions of the warrior's stone. It might fade slightly during the day when a majority of the demons rested, but come the next evening the emissions would return in increasing strength.

But the new stone worried him less than the warrior's stone in spite of its obvious presence. For he intended to have the new stone this very night, but the warrior's stone, zealously guarded by one who both knew what he had and yet had no idea, would continue to wreak havoc on the demons here. And they in turn would wreak havoc on those innocents around them.

Sudden motion beside a building alerted him; he had his hand on his sash knife before the preternaturally quick beings appeared before him, surrounding him, circling him. They jeered at him, their fangs already dripping blood and their otherwise human features distorted by demonic forehead and eyes.

He couldn't understand their words, but he knew they played with him. They had no use for *his* blood, after all.

"Don't be foolish," he told them, shifting so as to keep most of them in his sight as they danced around him, feinting with their makeshift clubs of broken wood. "This gains you nothing. Can't you feel the power of that which drives you?"

Not understanding, they laughed all the louder. As one, they leaped on him.

A Tuingas priest is not without his resources. Khundarr tucked his vulnerable long-nose in tight and stood braced and balanced, allowing the blows to pass by or bounce off—but none of the vampires rebounded without feeling the touch of his knife. The light blows didn't incapacitate the bullies . . . but the sight of all of them streaming blood while Khundarr stood untouched was enough to overcome the effects of the deathstone. The vampires exchanged a group glance and faded back into the night, not half so jeeringly as they'd come from it.

But Khundarr, although unharmed, was more affected than they could know. This tangible evidence of the deathstone's influence shook him badly. And it hardened a resolve already strong. Whatever it took, he would recover the raw stone tonight. Whatever.

Khundarr let the raw new stone pull him toward the location of the young Tuingas's death—a big building on a corner, with damaged doors that gave at his tug but then rebounded back into place.

After a moment's examination, he sliced through the bindings on the door handles. He didn't expect the violent *sproing!* of the highly stretchy ropes, but once he rubbed away the sting of the part that had snapped back to hit his hand, he forgot about them and stepped into the large room beyond.

The stone called to him. He found it halfway across the room, on a waist-high surface. It was immersed in a container of liquid with an over-whelmingly cheerful scent that almost contrived to cover the crucial scent of the deathstone itself.

All deathstones had the characteristic odor of their owners' dissolution, forever identifying them to family members by use of the specially devel-oped long-nose. The lysosomic self-destruction upon death had inspired the development of the deathstone in the first place. No Tuingas went any-where without a deathstone tucked into his stom-ach pouch behind the traditional sash. . . . The deathstone served not only as physical remains for family members, but a lingering memorial with impressions of the personality and death experi-ence of the individual.

To discover one thus, in the process of being ren-dered odorless, was sacrilege. Khundarr stiffened with his outrage. He quickly removed the stone from its bath, folding it into a heavily spell-inscribed leather wrapping that immediately muffled its emissions.

And then he realized someone was watching him. His long-nose, almost overwhelmed by the scent of the liquid, twitched reflexively toward the stairs. Something there gave a squeak of fear and shrank more tightly into the shadows.

A human. Possibly one of the humans who had done this abhorrent thing to a Tuingas deathstone. Khundarr growled deeply, knowing no single human was a match for a fully mature Tuingas, and no human could outwit a Tuingas long-nose no matter how he . . . no, this was a she . . . clung to darkness and crannies.

But he knew the girl would not be alone. Something in this dwelling had killed the young one; something in here might be strong enough to kill him, too. And then there would be yet another stone—another *raw* stone—loose in this world that was not prepared to deal with the ones it already had.

He tucked the temporarily protected stone into his own stomach pouch, growled a final invective toward the cowering creature near the stairs, and made his exit.

CHAPTER FOUR

Sleep was what Angel got . . . but not the quiet slumber he'd hoped for. He plunged instantly into dreams, dark and heavy and full of fury. *Wesley stood before him, book in hand, lecturing on the finer points of translating ancient demon languages. Angel ripped the book from him and then ripped the book in half—and then reached for Wesley.*

No. That's not right.

Lorne warbled away on the stage of Caritas. "You like me, you really like me," he said, full of emotion at the applause. Suddenly, badly rigged buckets of blood tipped over from above, showering Lorne in sticky redness. Lorne shouted, "Do the Dance of Joy!" and tipped his head back to lick his lips in glee—until Angel bounded onto the stage, shouting, "Mine! That's mine!" *and reached for Lorne—*

That's *really* not right. . . .

Cordelia—

Not Cordelia. Leave her alone!

Cordelia, dressed in an absurdly skimpy costume, carrying an armful of industry magazines and wearing an exaggerated pout. "They don't like me, none *of them like me—*" And then her eyes rolled back and she fell with a shriek, flinging magazines everywhere, shouting, "Vision! Vision! Vision!" *until he couldn't stand it anymore, all that guilt and resentment of guilt and the drama, and Angel reached for Cordelia—*

And his eyes flew open in the darkness of his bedroom. He didn't bolt upright in bed. He just lay there, the tremble of his body made all the more obvious by the stillness of his heart and lungs. He stared into the darkness at the dim definition of the ceiling, and thought, *Not again.*

Not again with the dreams, lurking in his nights and dragging at him during the day. Alienating him from his friends, turning his life into a living nightmare . . .

And then he did sit up, resting his elbows on the sheets that covered his cross-legged knees, and realizing suddenly *no, not again.* This was not Darla, enticing him with a drugged mix of fantasy and reality. This wasn't about luring him or manipulating him . . .

They were simply nightmares. Outpourings of anger, channeled through sleep. Anger, he suddenly realized, that didn't come from within. Some outside influence pounded at him, drawing on his own life, his own experience, to express itself.

But it was still anger he couldn't afford. Anger that could turn wrong, uncontrolled and leaving him with yet more regrets to overcome. He ground the heels of his hands against his eyes and said through gritted teeth, "Whoever you are, this isn't going to work." It wouldn't. He'd figure out who was doing this, he'd find them, and he'd put that anger to good use.

"Kittens," he murmured. "*Sesame Street*. Hula-Hoops. Kids' handprints in cement." But not those little Precious Moments statuettes, which always gave him an irresistible urge to smash things. "No, no, no . . . more kittens. And puppies." Yeah, the kind with all the wrinkles.

Better already.

But one thing was for sure: The others couldn't know. Couldn't even guess. If they even suspected there were dreams attached to this evening's mood . . .

For all he knew, they'd stake him just to get it over with.

Not really. Surely that was just an indulgent bit of self-pity creeping in.

Except he knew he'd already pushed them to the limit . . . and beyond. "Big Bird!" he said with much determination.

Not until much later did it occur to him that he

hadn't come out of the nightmares on his own. In this hotel with its broken doors and habitually unpredictable visitors, something had woken him from that unnaturally deep sleep . . . and then slunk silently away.

"Okay, so this is strange," Cordelia said to no one in particular, standing at the hotel's front doors. One was as Gunn had left it, but the other hung open, cardboard half-ripped from the broken glass, which still jabbed toward the center of the door in jagged shards. A thoroughly slashed bungee cord hung over the handle . . . and on the floor . . . and on the stair rail . . . and she thought she saw a piece out in the lobby. Nasty business, cutting a bungee cord under tension.

She took a step into the hotel. "Hello?"

No answer. But she was expecting that. Gunn never got here this early. Fred was no doubt here somewhere, but not predictable about showing up. Even Wes rarely appeared this early, unless they had a hot and heavy case under way—in which case he usually simply hadn't gone home. In fact, if she'd gotten an answer . . . *then* she'd start to worry. Still, better safe than demon fodder. She took another cautious step. "Hello? Anyone here? Any unwanted visitors from other dimensions, master vampires out to rule the world, mayors with a snake fetish?"

Just silence.

"Well, good then. Because I'm really not in the mood for it. In fact, I'm *never* in the mood—oh." Sometime during her peer around the lobby, Angel had come padding down the stairs. *Way* too early for Angel. So early, in fact, that he'd even forgotten to get dressed and now stood bare-chested, looking at her in a vaguely startled way. Just in case he should get fully the idea that her openmouthed stare was anything more than utter surprise at seeing him emerge before late afternoon, she said flatly, "Well, hubba-hubba."

He didn't appear to notice. He looked around the lobby, from courtyard doors to weapons case to the counter to her, and it didn't seem to her like he was all there. He said, "I thought I heard something."

"Right. That would have been me. Just taking morning head-count. Not meaning that literally, of course, though around here you never—"

"No, not you. Earlier. During the night."

"Are you listening to yourself?" she said, dumping her purse and light sweater on one of the roundchairs. "Because I am, and let me tell you, it's not an enlightening experience." But then her glance fell on the plastic butter tub—economy size—that held the weird ugly stone from the demon goo. That *should* have held the weird ugly stone, but now only held the remains of the Nature's Miracle in which it had been soaking. "Hey, the stone-thing is gone."

"What's gone?" he said, and suddenly he was

right beside her, and *boy* didn't she hate it when he did that. His gaze landed on the slashed bungees and darkened. "I *did* hear something. Someone broke in here last night."

"Stands to follow, since the stone-thing is gone and those bungee bits are all over the place," Cordelia said with what she thought was just the right touch of sarcasm.

"Stone-thing," he repeated.

"*Yes,*" she said, waving a hand at the butter tub. "The one that Dissolvo Demon left behind that Wesley was soaking so we could even get close enough to figure ou—ow, ow, ow!"

—crates of lettuce weird little colorful Muppet demon people laughing no people screaming no people dying blowgun blowgun blowgun—

"Oh," said Fred, in her most tentative voice. Probably the only voice in the world that wouldn't shatter Cordelia's head right at this moment. *No one else say anything oh please.*

She was on the floor, of course. Or on the stairs. Something uneven. And she considered opening her eyes, but even the faintest glimmer of light sliced into her head like shards from the broken door.

"Oh," Fred said again. And though she was trying to sound casual, she instead sounded shaken. Why, Cordelia couldn't imagine, since *hers* was the head being stirred. "I didn't realize . . . that is, I'm sorry. Hardly anyone's ever down here at this hour. But that's probably why you're here, isn't it? To find privacy."

Privacy? That was enough to get Cordelia's eyes open, slicing knives of light or no. She'd fallen toward the stairs all right, but she was *on* Angel.

"You okay?" he asked, as if he hadn't even noticed. *Men.*

As quickly as possible, Cordelia removed herself from lap and bare skin territory and sat on genuine stair, leaning against a railing that was a weird combination of art deco and dignity. She tucked really short hair back behind her ear, finding once again that in disoriented moments like these, she still expected her hair to be long and dark. "I'm fine," she said. "As fine as anyone would be with all this dungeon of horror stuff going on in her skull." She took a deep breath, said, "Looked like Terminal Market. There was some little demon guy, reminded me of a Muppet. And people were laughing at him, and he just went crazy . . . throwing lettuce and then he had this blowgun and people were screaming. . . ."

"I remember Muppets," Fred said, as if in wonder.

"Muppets," Angel said, sounding strangely unnerved. He got to his feet, finally seemed to realize his state of partial undress, and crossed his arms across his chest—then uncrossed them and tried it the other way. Didn't cover any more territory that way and gave up on it.

Impatient, Cordelia staggered to her feet and went to grope through her purse, hunting migraine killers. "Yeah, yeah. A cross between Kermit the Frog and Beaker."

"Beaker was my favorite," Fred told them. She sat midway down the stairs with her arms wrapped around her knees. Not taking up very much room, as usual, her fine brown hair drawn in two low ponytails behind her ears, baby doll T-shirt and jeans hidden by an oversized open-front sweater. "I like the idea of a Muppetish demon. It sounds a lot better than what was sneaking around here earlier." She shuddered, and hugged her arms tightly.

"Here?" Angel said, an edge creeping into his voice. "Earlier as in yesterday, which of course we all know about, or earlier as in this morning, which we all *ought* to know about? Why didn't you wake me?"

"*Angel,*" Cordelia said, frozen in mid–pill hunt first by Fred's revelation and then by Angel's demanding reaction.

"I tried to wake you!" Fred said, drawing more tightly around herself, her eyes going a little wider, a lot more alarmed. "Really I did. But then it saw me—or I think it saw me—and I was afraid to move. It seemed mad. From the way it growled, I mean."

Curiouser and curiouser. Cordelia pinned Angel

with a look. "I guess you slept through a lot. Not usual."

With all the deftness of a hippo on ice, he side-stepped the unasked question, still looking at Fred. "Okay, you tried to wake me, but you were afraid. Still . . . you had to have seen whoever came in here."

"Or *whatever*," Cordelia added.

Fred squirmed slightly. "I'm not sure."

"This is such a great morning so far," Angel said. "Isn't it a great morning?"

"Ignore him," Cordelia told Fred, and finally found the pills she wanted. She did a quick calculation of headache intensity against need for consciousness and broke the pill in half with her hands in her purse. Hardly subtle. But it was amazing what people didn't see when you didn't act like whatever you were up to was any big deal.

"It's just that it was still kinda dark. And I was up here. Trying to wake Angel, you know. I guess I didn't knock loud enough, but usually . . . you know, he hears everything. And then I was preferring to be not seen, and that kinda meant not being where it could see me . . ." She hesitated, and her voice took on the unaccustomed note of certainty that reared up every now and then and made Cordelia wonder if there wasn't more to Fred than frightened and traumatized little cave girl after all. "Not Muppetish," she said firmly. "Big. And it knew what it wanted. It went right over to the counter and then it left."

"Demon chases man, demon dies," Angel muttered. "Leaves behind the ugly stone. Demon Two steals the ugly stone. Way too many things we don't know about here."

"Okay," Cordelia said, thinking more of Fred's remarks than Angel's mumbling. "We can work with that." They wouldn't get much from it, but it was more than they'd known before. "Meanwhile, let's not forget about Terminal Market, okay? Vision Girl is not to be ignored."

"Call Gunn and Wesley," Angel said, and then gave her a second glance from beneath a brow that seemed to be warring between concerned and preoccupied. "Or do you need to go lie down?"

"I'm sure I'll be fine," she said, proving that she was just as good as he, in her own way, of dodging direct answers. "Just go get dressed. And hurry. We'll solve the mystery of the missing ugly stonething when I don't have screaming people in my head, okay?"

Vision Girl was not to be argued with either.

CHAPTER FIVE

Wesley and Gunn headed down Seventh Street in the getting-uncomfortable warmth of mid-morning. Angel himself ran the underground, ever in consideration of how bursting into flame could ruin his day. This particular day already had enough strikes against it . . . the dreams, the lingering sense of constant prodding by someone else's emotions . . . Cordelia's questions. She knew him best, and while he might fool the others for a while . . .

He'd stay out of Cordelia's way.

He knew of several exits into the warehouses of the produce district; Wesley and Gunn found him lurking in the slightly arched truck drive-through of a warehouse, staring across sunlight asphalt to the neighboring warehouse. There, perched on the upper corner of a stack of metal melon crates, was the very Slith demon who had taunted him in Caritas.

"Odd," Wesley said, squinting out at the demon with a thoughtful frown. "The Slith don't usually come out in daylight. They're very shy. And they certainly don't cause trouble or draw attention to themselves. Are we sure this is what Cordelia meant?"

"Terminal Market, Muppetish demon," Angel said. "What part have we got wrong so far?"

"None, I'm sorry to say."

Gunn moved uneasily beside them. "Look," he said. "Even if this isn't from Cordy's vision, it's not *right*. We need to do something about it before someone gets hurt."

"I should think the only one in real danger is the Slith demon." Wesley let his crossbow drop. "Without a blowgun, they're virtually harmless—unless you count bad table manners."

"Tell me about it," Angel said. The slug-sprayed leather duster would be at the cleaners for days. "But Cordelia mentioned—"

"Blowgun," Gunn interrupted, succinct and tense, his gaze riveted on the Slith and his newly apparent weapon. "*Not* harmless."

And now someone had noticed the little demon, and drew aside a vendor in a stained apron to point and question and laugh, obviously taking the being's presence as some sort of prank—although just as obviously, the demon didn't like being laughed at.

"These people live too close to Hollywood," Angel muttered.

"Yes, and now they're in trouble," Wesley said as the Slith gestured vehemently at the gathering crowd. It ripped a flyer off the crate and shredded it with quick efficiency. "I hate to see the Slith hurt—but these people are going to get killed—"

"Killed?" Gunn snorted. "He's making *spitballs*."

"Yes, which he'll then rub in his armpit, where his poison-generating glands will turn the spitballs into lethal projectiles."

Gunn gave the Slith an assessing look, and winced. "That's just plain nasty."

"I still don't understand why—," Wesley started, but shook his head. "I suppose it doesn't matter. He's out there, and we've got to stop him."

But Angel thought he might understand. He didn't know the how or the why . . . but he understood. Take a vampire with a soul, one who understands darkness and anger and killing . . . one who constantly fights his past and the barely controlled demon within. Then take a quiet little creature who likes to suck on cinnamon-flavored slugs and go to bed early.

Introduce an outside source of anger.

Nothing new to Angel. But if it was affecting other demons as well . . . demons who had no experience with the dark extremes of their nature . . .

"We could have a problem," he muttered to himself.

The others gave him a strange look in stereo. Wesley said, "I think we've established that."

On the crate, the Slith dropped into a sudden crouch and put the reedy blowgun to what passed for its lips. No one shrieked or ran; no one seemed to suspect there was any danger at all. Angry Slith on one side; notorious vampire on the other.

Except—unlike the Slith—Angel still wore his do-good clothes. Tattered around the edges and no doubt a little thin right now, but . . . he stepped up to the edge of the shadow and flung his arms wide. "Hey!" he bellowed, startling everyone in the crowd; they looked at him with the kind of wary regard they might well have given the Slith had they been wiser. "I've been looking for you! Angel sent me."

"He never!" the demon squealed back, a second surprise for the crowd. *It speaks!* But it lowered the blowgun to listen.

"They're realizing he's a little too articulate for a publicity puppet," Wesley said, casually keeping his crossbow out of sight now that they'd been spotted by crowd and Slith alike. He smiled, a very British royal-smile-to-the-crowd expression, and added through his teeth, "I'm not sure if that's good or bad . . . they'll either run for cover or gather to gawk . . ."

"It's L.A.," Gunn said, making no particular effort to acknowledge the crowd at all. "I vote on gawking."

Angel kept his eyes on the demon, on the blow-gun that could so easily come back into play. Not the time to lose the Slith's attention. He shouted, "You calling me a liar?"

"What are you doing?" Wesley said, his voice low—for no particular purpose, since the rising reaction of the crowd certainly covered anything in the range of normal conversation.

"Taking his attention away from the crowd," Angel said, leaving *of course* unspoken . . . although he wondered if just possibly his judgment had been affected by those same subtle waves of negativity that messed with the Slith. If truly . . . he was just looking for a fight. "Unless you want to shove your way through all those people to get to him, by which time he'd be gone?"

"You're a liar!" the Slith screamed at him. "You said you were Angel!"

"You going somewhere with this?" Gunn asked, also under his breath . . . but with that tone that meant he was restraining himself rather than try-ing to be discreet. "Because it looks like trouble to me."

"Trust me," Angel said, not turning away from the sunlit gathering and the furious little demon—and not sure he could do the same were their situations

ations reversed. By now the crowd was watching the byplay, heads swiveling back and forth in unison, currently focused on Angel as Angel told the creature, "I *am* Angel!"

The Slith sputtered something inarticulate and gestured with the blowgun, finally sputtering out, "Lie! Lie! Angel is my friend! You—you—*booger-head!*"

Gunn said, "Ouch. That's gotta hurt."

Touched by some of the same driving darkness that had so overwhelmed the Slith, Angel struggled to find just the right response. "Bite me!" he shouted.

Maybe that wasn't it.

Or maybe it was, because the Slith lost it. He pounded the wire cabbage crates and screamed nastiness and put the blowgun to his lips—but by then the crowd was scattering, people shoving and pushing and cursing as they sensed an end to the benign moments of this terribly odd encounter.

A sticky spitball *thwapped* into Angel's jacket, stuck there a moment, and rolled down a few inches.

"Don't touch that!" Wesley told him, as if Angel had any intention of touching a spitball that had been rolled in demon armpit even if it *hadn't* been poisoned.

"Incoming!" Gunn cried, but Angel glanced back up to see that he didn't mean *incoming spitball*. He meant *incoming demon*. Faster even than he'd been in Caritas, bounding forward and pro-pelled by rage, the Slith hurtled into Angel at chest height, knocking him right off his feet.

As he hit the ground, stunned, Wesley cried, "Sun, sun!" It made sudden sense when he felt his skin start to sizzle, right there where his pant leg pulled up in the scuffle to expose his ankle. But Wes and Gunn grabbed his jacket at the shoulders and pulled him back, opting to save him from the sun rather than the demon who pummeled inef-fectively at his face.

Angel finally managed to swat the Slith off, mak-ing a cat-like roll to his feet even as he grabbed the Slith's rubbery scruff and held him up off the ground.

"Now *that* was a girlie fight," Gunn announced.

Wesley preoccupied himself with a search of the asphalt around them. "Where is it?" he said. "We can't just leave it here." He glanced at Angel. "Do you still have it?"

Holding the squalling demon out away from himself, Angel looked down at his jacket. There was a clear trail where the spitball had rolled down the leather—a sticky line already gathering dust. But no spitball. "Hey," he said, giving the Slith a little shake, feeling its squalls beat against him just like the inexplicable emotions that drove it. Face it, drove them *both*. "I got the demon. *You* get the poison spitball."

"Angel, this is no joke. We can't—"

"Wesley," Angel interrupted, his voice going hard in a reflection of that outside emotion, the angerhatekill he felt so keenly. "Do I look like I'm joking?"

There was a moment of silence as even the Slith stopped his struggle to watch Wesley's reaction. Angel winced inside. In the street, the crowd began to creep back in. Still curious, still not quite believing they'd actually seen any of what they'd indeed seen. He didn't want to give them any more evidence. By now, someone probably had a vid-cam.

"No," Wesley said after a long and considered moment, his serious features even more serious than usual, his eyes icy blue-gray and shadowed at the same time. "I don't suppose you do."

"I'm taking him back to Caritas before this turns into a sideshow," Angel said. Back to the tunnels, safe in their shadows. And into Lorne's club, where a demon might have to put up with bad singing, but could be sure no one else would do it deliberate harm. The Furies had seen to that, with their spell against demon violence within the club.

"Too late to avoid the sideshow," Gunn said, indicating the crowd. "But if you don't get out of here, it'll get worse."

With a glance to make sure the poison spitball was indeed not still clinging to his person, Angel left Wesley and Gunn to find it, taking along their more obvious weapons in one hand and the Slith in the other. After a few moments underground, it said sullenly, "Put me down, big bully. I'll come."

"Uh-huh," Angel said, and kept walking. The Slith erupted into a frenzy of name-calling and futile wiggling, and after a moment hung limply again. Angel pretended that his arm wasn't starting to ache. He took the turn that would get him to the underground entrance at Caritas, carefully stepping around the occasional blotches of sunlight from open gratings. The sunburn on his ankle still stung. Eventually he asked, "You seen your friend today?"

"*Real* Angel? Wouldn't tell *you*."

Angel stopped walking and looked straight at the Slith's moody features. Crocodile eyes, half closed in an angry squint. Broad, triangular mouth so pursed with disapproval, it seemed likely to cause cheek muscle cramps. "Has it occurred to you that your behavior at that little scene was hardly Slith-like? That it even could have gotten you killed? That maybe I even saved your life? That there's something going on here that's bigger than you and me and *where's Angel?*"

The Slith looked back at him. If possible, its mouth pursed even a little more.

"Fine," Angel said. "Has it occurred to you that I can bash you against this concrete wall with pretty much no effort at all?"

The Slith's gaze slanted over to the wall, back to Angel, and then to the wall again. "Haven't seen him. He's got a busy schedule. *Real* work."

"And do you just happen to know what he's working *on?*"

Those little eyes glanced again at the wall, "Not to say."

Angel got the sense the creature spoke truthfully, but he persisted. "Something to do with a guy and a bowling ball bag. And maybe demons that don't hang around long after you kill them."

The Slith's pursed mouth relaxed in surprise. "There has been this man, yes. Just a stupid human, not important. Don't know demons."

Angel hesitated, knowing he'd reached that point where he'd either have to accept the Slith's story or indulge in a little bashing . . . except that he really *wanted* to do the bashing, which was way too wrong. And he had the distinct feeling that if he started bashing, he just might not be able to stop.

Maybe Lorne could do better.

"Hey," the Slith protested as Angel headed down the tunnel again. "I spoke! Put me down!"

"When we're inside Caritas," Angel said. "And when you're all comfy in a long-term chair. When Lorne says you're safe to go, you can go. But it's gonna involve singing, so I'd start picking out my favorites if I were you."

• • •

Lorne eyed the Slith with a bleary gaze. "You brought him here . . . why, again? Sweetstuff, do I have *permanent sucker* written on my forehead?"

Angel hesitated, couldn't help a glance at the forehead in question. "Not visibly." He indicated at the sullen Slith. It sat on a bar stool with its gawky knees up by its ears and its thin wrists cable-tied together, sucking on a mollifying slug. "This is the one place he can't get into trouble."

"Hmm," Lorne said flatly. "An original idea if I ever heard one." He gave the club floor a distinct glance, and Angel followed it, for the first time taking in the unusual state of affairs. That he'd been blind to it before now made him wince inside; it only proved his distraction with the anger that thumped at his chest. *In* his chest, as though it had taken the place of his not-beating heart.

No one had claimed the stage—that was strange right there—but the tables overflowed with demons of all shapes and sizes. Unhappy demons and demon mixed-breeds who clung to their chairs as if they were safety nets and eyed their neighbors warily.

"I told you, nasty mojo," Lorne said, lowering his voice. He gave Angel a once-over as obvious as a stage whisper and said, "This time I *know* you feel it." The Slith leaned closer to hear, and Lorne pushed him away without looking, his broad green hand clashing badly with the demon's rubbery blue face. He nodded at his customers. "They're all afraid of what might happen out there. Or of what they might do."

"Our little friend here has already *done* it . . . this is the best place for him. Along with most any of us, I'd say." Angel, too, felt the relief. The relief of knowing no matter his anger, no matter his control—or lack thereof—in here, he was incapable of hurting anyone.

Too bad he couldn't stay.

"I don't suppose you know?" Lorne said. "*Someone's* got to."

"What's going on?" Angel shook his head. "I can tell you that it's not hitting humans. The others . . . they've noticed something's up, but they're all at their normal level of cranky."

"Well, I'm telling you what, hon-buns. If this keeps up, I'm going to slip myself a Mickey and go into hibernation until it's all over."

Angel gave him a sharp look. "Can you?"

A walking stick of a demon approached the bar and plunked down his empty glass, gesturing a desire for more.

"Go away," Lorne told it. "I'm having a *me* moment."

The demon gave this statement silent thought and seemed about to protest, but looked around the club and reconsidered. The very number of customers made it clear that this was the place to be . . . with or without service. It ambled away, leaving Lorne free to say, "Can I what? Hibernate? I only wish. But when the emotional leakage around here gets too rough—trust me, I can fake it." He reached under the bar to produce a pre-mixed pitcher of something so garish, it made a perfect counterpoint to his suit. "A couple of these will do the trick. You note I have them ready."

"I did, actually," Angel said. "Note that, I mean." He raked another glance over the crowded room and steeled himself to leave it. To go back out where he had only himself to control . . . himself. "If you pick up anything useful . . ."

"Yeah, yeah, I'll call. I've got an interest here."

"And him," Angel said, nodding at the Slith. "He stays. Until we figure this out."

Lorne gave a mournful glance at the club, which was already showing the wear and tear of a capacity crowd. "I think they're *all* here to stay," he said, and looked longingly at the garish pitcher. But his natural inclinations won out; he cocked an eyebrow at the Slith and said, "Sing something for me. Or hum. If you hum, it's got to be longer."

The Slith gave him an intrigued look, its gator eyes going bright. It cleared its throat and began humming, a throbbingly nasal, wandering pitch that was quite clearly supposed to be *something* and just as clearly . . . wasn't.

Lorne winced. "Ow," he said. "Bad."

Angel said, "What did you get?"

"Nothing more than I'm getting from any of the others—nebulous feelings of anger, a readiness to act on them, and a certain amount of puzzlement about the whole thing," Lorne said, massaging his temple. "It's just really *bad* humming."

"Boogerhead," the Slith informed him primly, apparently including everyone within hearing distance. He took a healthy bite of slug and turned his back on them.

Angel thought he probably had the right idea.

"What's with you?" Cordelia said as Angel stalked through the lobby. She stood by the hotel doors, prodding the temporary plywood boards she'd just paid good money to have installed and wondering when the hotel would take another round of damage.

He didn't mince words or waste pleasantries. "I've got armpit poison on my jacket."

"Ohhh-kay," she said. "Gotta love that segue." *Segue*, a really good actress word to know for scene transitions and all that. She pointed at the front desk. "That pet accident stuff is behind there. I decided there was no point in letting it get all the way back to the maintenance closet. Where're Gunn and Wesley?"

"Coming back any minute, if they didn't get into

any more trouble." He pulled out the cleaner and the rag she'd looped through its handle. "I've never seen Caritas that crowded."

"Lack of segue, total nonsequitur . . . you sure you don't have anything on your mind?" She left the doors to look at him more closely as he dabbed Nature's Miracle on his coat.

"Just all the answers we *don't* have," he said, and gave her his own close look, an inspection so intense that for a sudden startling instant she felt like he could see right through her. Just as she realized she was holding her breath, he said, "How about you? Anything on your mind? Visions? Glimpses? Even little ones?"

She shook her head, not trusting her voice—and then frowned, crossing her arms in fake defiance, more than a little shaken by that look. What did he think he'd see? And what drove him to look so hard for it? "You expecting something?"

He shook his head, just as suddenly distracted again. "Have a feeling."

She narrowed her eyes, totally annoyed by his cryptic mood and by her reaction to it. "Maybe you should keep it to yourself, then. Until you feel like making sense or something."

The door flung open with an emphatic bang, startling Cordelia—and to judge by their expressions as they entered the hotel, Wesley and Gunn as well. She winced and said, "Another entrance like that and you'll take them right off their hinges. Where they barely are to begin with, you may have noticed."

"Sorry," Wesley said. "All that adrenaline from a successful round of demon-hunting, you know."

"Besides which, they looked fixed," Gunn added.

"Did you find it?" Angel asked, tossing the rag back behind the counter.

"Find what?" Cordelia asked. "Is everyone talking in code today?"

"Well . . . perhaps we weren't so much demon-hunting as . . ."

Gunn grinned. "Spitball hunting. And yes, we found it. Disposed of it. You?"

"Left him at Caritas, getting hum therapy and hating it. You ever heard a Slith hum?" Angel raised a hand. "Never mind. Just don't."

Wesley turned to Cordelia. "And you?"

She gestured impatiently at the door. "What part of those newly boarded doors didn't you see? You think some guy just came out of nowhere to do that? I've been doing my part." She left her mouth open to mention the migraine, but closed it before the words came out. Getting attention and comfort was good, but those strange worried looks they tended to cast her way only added to the burden of the whole vision thing.

"Stranger things have happened," Wesley said.

"It's just we *do* need to get a fix on that demon to have any understanding of the encounters. Especially now that we've lost the"—he looked at the empty butter tub and finished lamely—"ugly stone."

"Be my guest." She pointed him to the new identification book, left facedown on the front desk. He winced and rushed to rescue it, running a thumb along the spine as she said, "In order to use that thing, you've got to have details. Sure, there's a choice for five appendages, but you've got to know what kind that fifth one is—is it spatulate or palmate, tubular or fringed . . ."

"Ouch," said Gunn.

"I see your point," Wesley said. He inserted a piece of paper into the book and returned it to her. Cordelia glanced at it. Some old notepaper with the zoo logo, no doubt soon to be appropriate for actual note-taking on her part. "Still, perhaps we'll gather more data."

"Be nice if we did that *before* another of them comes in here wrecking things," Gunn observed, resting an elbow on the counter. "Especially if it's going to do a smelly meltdown when we kill it."

Assuming it didn't get one of them first. But that was a factor they all lived with, every day. They just didn't say it out loud very often. Cordelia sighed and ran a hand through her short hair. "I think we need to find that man," she said. "The demon was after *him*. Or else we should find that guy who looked like Angel. I'll bet he knows something."

Angel instantly protested, "He didn't look *anything* like me."

"We need to find him, anyway," Gunn said.

Cordelia felt it coming, like a mental sneeze. An incredibly painful mental—

Joggers. Brown hair, ponytails, mother and daughter running together blood and bright yellow skin, screaming—always screaming—

"San Vincente Boulevard," she gasped from the floor. "That median park the joggers use. There's this yellow guy with a weird mohawk not-hair and these knives . . . growing . . . from its arms—"

"*Miquot?*" Wesley said. "Hunting joggers on the strip park is hardly up to their standards."

"I wouldn't call this hunting," Cordelia said, pressing her fingers to her temples. Oh, ow. Shouldn't there be some rule about no more than one vision per day? She was sure there should be a rule. . . . "More like . . . savaging. And . . ." She frowned, trying to grasp the most elusive part of the vision, the feel of it, the things that really didn't come through as *vision* at all. Someone grasped her elbows from behind and lifted her to her feet, all but carrying her to one of the roundchairs. *Angel.* None of the others had that casual strength. "I don't know how . . . but this is related to the Terminal Market thing."

"To the Slith demon?" Wesley asked, incredulous.

"Yes," she said, more assertive as the first shrieking pain receded into pounding waves. "And by something other than the fact that neither job is going to pay. I don't know what yet . . . and I wouldn't waste any time getting to those joggers."

"This one's yours," Angel said, *though—was that regret?* Cordelia narrowed her eyes. Yes, he very much looked as if he'd be fine with tearing into some Miquot.

"Yes," Wesley said. "The broad daylight and all."

"Don't worry," Cordelia said, wincing. "The way the day is going, I'll have something else for you soon."

She wished she thought she was wrong.

CHAPTER SIX

Angel went back to the underground. Back to sewers and utility tunnels and areas that none of L.A.'s city planners ever envisioned . . . or even knew about. The perfect place to ponder dark thoughts, to let them pound home the knowledge . . . *I've got to figure out what's going on. I've got to stop it.* But with no direct line of inquiry and with Wesley and Gunn handling the Miquot and jogger incident and Cordelia napping off her vision in a second-floor room, Angel did what the others expected. He turned back to the matter of the unidentified demon-turned-goo-in-the-lobby and the scrawny excuse for a vampire wanna-be who'd copped Angel's wardrobe.

It still made no sense to him. Imitation as an indication of admiration . . . admiration of *what?* A young mortal's callow irresponsibility, a hundred-plus of unspeakable evil, and almost a hundred years of living off rats? A few recent years of playing the good guy hardly made up for any of that. And the last thing he wanted was the responsibility of knowing someone else—*anyone* else—was using him as a template.

None of the denizens of the underground he spoke to seemed to think much of it one way or the other.

"Amateur," snorted the highly humanized male Angel stopped not far from the hotel. He and his date were dressed for dinner out, wearing muckers and carrying their dress shoes through the sewers. "I heard something about it. He's just a pretender."

"Needs to be eaten," said the hunchbacked Oua'shin demon crouched against the side of a sewer tunnel, gnawing on something furry. He paused to insert a long claw into his mouth and withdrew part of a stretchy pet collar. "Just making trouble for us all, not keeping the right profile, drawing attention."

"Needs to spend a little time in a hellmouth," growled an elderly hybrid with a face that hadn't matched even before its human aspects had collapsed with time.

• • •

But they didn't know where to find him. Or if they did, they weren't admitting it . . . and Angel wasn't ready to create resentment by switching from questions to intimidation.

Not yet.

No doubt the fake Angel had a small dingy cubby of an apartment somewhere. Possibly he had a pathetic pavement-scraping job and only threw on his Angel-making duds in his off time as his escape from banality to excitement. Angel spent a moment envisioning the man in dirty coveralls, picking up trash from some community facility or fast-food parking lot, a colorless being going unnoticed in the human world.

A shrill ringing noise startled him, echoing off the cement walls of the sewer on the way back to the hotel. *The cell phone.* For once, he had it; for once, he had it turned on. Somewhere . . .

He patted himself down, finally snagged it out of the inside pocket of his jacket, and fumbled it open. "Yeah?" he said, trying to sound like he'd been busy and successful instead of daydreaming in a sewer after getting nowhere.

"Vision," Cordelia said, sounding frantic even over the hollow tones of the cell phone. "Sewer. Kid looking for his cat. About to get eaten."

"Where?"

"Sewer!"

"Lots of those to choose from," he reminded

her, thinking sourly that all his weapons were at the hotel. This was supposed to be an amiable question-and-answer expedition, not another visionquest. "There's gotta be something distinctive about it—"

"No, there doesn't," she shot back at him in the sort of strained whisper that meant she'd probably be raising her voice into that higher register if she didn't have a splitting vision-headache. Or several of them. "Just find—"

The phone gave a forlorn beep and died. Angel scowled at it, a serious scowl that lesser life-forms would have known to flee.

The phone remained unimpressed.

Great. Kid, about to be eaten. Here in the extensive sewer system—at least he knew that much, and could stay out of utilities access and informal tunnels—with no clue *where*.

Except for his memory of the Oua'shin demon picking a pet collar out of his mouth.

Kid. Looking for his cat.

Angel ran.

And then stopped. That couldn't be it. The hunchbacked Oua'shin hunted close to the ground . . . and they hunted animals, not humans. They never went above; never confronted humanity in any way.

A thin scream cut through the damp tunnel air.

Couldn't be it. *Was.*

He ran with a vampire's speed.

The screaming would have guided him had memory not done the trick. He took a sharp corner, came upon the struggle—a dark-skinned boy, maybe six years old, skinny and flailing and panicked. The Oua'shin, clutching him with an expression of manic fury.

On the floor beside a still-rocking flashlight, something furry and bloody, an elongated lump with pearly jagged leg bone jutting out the end—

Angel scooped it up on the run, used his strength and anger and momentum to shove it through the Oua'shin's gummy black eye. The demon stiffened, flinging his arms and legs wide in a death spasm. The kid squirted free.

Angel kept his head turned, waiting the instant it took to repress fang-face before letting the kid see him.

Except it wouldn't go away. His own rage coursed through him, freed by the incident, startling in intensity, fogging his brain . . .

The kid cried. A weak, tasty sound . . .

Repulsed by his own reaction, Angel startled himself back into human visage. He gave himself another moment, made sure of it—and turned to the boy.

"Spike!" the child cried.

Angel wheeled around to search the darkness

beyond the flickering flashlight beam, his eye
targeting an image of the lean, bleach-headed
vampire—but no. Not here.

Spike the *cat*. The boy's pet.

Deliberately, Angel put his foot over the collar
almost hidden in a shallow puddle. "He's not here,"
he said. "Let's get you back aboveground."

The boy's smeared face took on an obstinate
expression. "I saw him here. He hunts them big
old rats."

"It's a big place," Angel said simply. "He's not
here, here."

Or most of him wasn't.

Angel fought the sudden impulse to say, *Look,
kid, the cat's lying all around you in little bits and
pieces, with most of him stuck between this demon's
teeth. He's not coming back home*, ever, *so get your
butt moving!* Instead, extra gently, he held out his
hand. "Let's go. I think you need a Band-Aid or two,
and I have some with Blue from *Blue's Clues*."

That produced an extra-loud snuffle, as if the
boy suddenly realized he indeed had a scratch here
and there. He said doubtfully, "You do?"

Not really. They belonged to Cordelia. "I definitely do." He retrieved the flashlight, and by the
time he straightened he had a little boy clinging to
his other hand. Ignoring the sweet smell of young
blood, he led the boy back out to the early evening
streets.

"We're in trouble if we've got to jog this whole strip." Gunn climbed out of his truck at the parking lot in the area defined by Pico and Venice and La Brea— and San Vincente itself, which held the median strip part that originated right here. He wished he'd chosen footwear that was less street commando and more joggerly. Then again, he wished he knew why the Miquot was riled up in the first place . . . and most of all he wished he knew why Cordelia had the faint smudge of worry on her brow when she looked at Angel. Of all of them, she knew him best . . . if *she* was worried, Gunn was worried.

Wesley exited the passenger side and slammed the door. "We won't be the only ones in trouble," he said. "Joggers up against a Miquot . . . I can't imagine what would possess a Miquot to stoop to such an easy target."

"Take it easy on the door." Gunn shot him a scowl and added, "And how can a demon be possessed?"

"Just a figure of speech." Wesley looked down at his loafers, then looked at Gunn over the hood of the truck. "Not that I don't appreciate this fine parking job, but . . ."

"You thought we were going to cruise the strip park?" Gunn asked. "Sure, maybe we can go slow enough in the left lane to incite an L.A. freeway shoot-out. That'd be a nice break from Miquot."

"It's hardly the freeway," Wesley said, in patient mode, opening his door again.

"People have tempers everywhere," Gunn said, climbing back into the truck. "Or hadn't you noticed lately? Anyway, she'd better not get so much as scratched." He patted the dashboard and waited for the chance to pull onto San Vincente so they could prowl along the green strip with its random trees and regular bisections of slanting left-turn lanes.

"Just drive," Wesley said, an edge finally creeping into his voice. "I'll watch the median. Oh, and roll down that window."

"The better to hear their screaming," Gunn muttered. More innocents in the way of trouble . . . he wasn't sure why L.A. didn't wise up.

Because Miquot don't attack joggers.

Not usually.

No, *usually* they were more of a tough bounty hunter type, going in for the big game, growing their own knives from their arms at will and taking on what challenged them.

Uneasily, he wondered what else might be going on in L.A., what other *not usual* things were coming down just as he started a fresh batch of kids as neighborhood demon watch. A fresh batch of cocky, overconfident kids who present him with the opposite problem Angel faced in his impersonator. *These* kids were so full of themselves that they didn't leave room for seeing how someone else went about it. They were ready to strike out on their own, make their own names . . . and if he didn't get them turned around, meeting their own dire fates.

Yeah, bad timing.

"Is that—?" Wesley said, pointing across the steering wheel at a flash of yellow. Someone behind them honked, then pulled around to pass on the right, gesturing nastily.

That particular shade of yellow, the way the figure clung to the trees and shadows . . . "Looks like it," Gunn said, jerking the truck into a left-turn lane and ignoring the horn that sounded behind him. He bumped up on the grass, half-on, half-off the road, and cut the engine. "Plan?" he asked, groping in the space behind the seat for their weapons bag.

Wesley held up the crossbow he'd prepared, and a handful of bolts. "Turn him into a pincushion from afar. Then, when he notices—"

"You got enough bolts there so he'll bother to notice?" Gunn asked dryly.

Wesley ignored him in a dogged way. "Then he should be weakened enough that between the two of us—"

Decisive, Gunn said, "I'm bringing more bolts. *And* another crossbow. I'll load, you shoot. If we're going to pincushion him, let's do it right."

"Fine." Wesley hopped out of the truck as the first scream broke through the traffic noise. He headed for it at a run.

Gunn hesitated, and then followed his impulse to grab the entire weapons bag and bring it along.

These Miquot . . . too nasty to take any plan for granted.

Hefting the crossbow and weapons bag, Gunn sprinted after Wesley, the sparse trees and cars a blur to either side. *Damn thing ought to have chosen a better spot.* One that wasn't so out in the open, where so many once-blithe people could witness the previously unbelievable.

Where two innocent women weren't playing a horrifying game of keep-away from a yellow, fin-headed killing machine. Gunn could see them clearly now—enough to know they hadn't wasted time trying to understand what attacked them or why; they'd split up, working to defend each other, not with strength so much as distraction. Brown hair up in saucy jogger's ponytails, matching outfits . . . mother-daughter team. As Gun and Wesley reached decent crossbow range, the Miquot closed in on the daughter, and the mother kicked it and ran. The Miquot whirled to follow.

That's not right. Miquot were not stupid; they were not distractable. They were dangerous, intelligent, and cunning and as well-trained as any

Slayer. Gunn set the crossbow to his shoulder; Wesley's twanged beside him, and the first bolt buried itself in the Miquot. Gunn aimed and—

—*thwap*—

—his bolt sprouted from the Miquot's arm. "Hah," Gunn said. "Try growing more knives from that—"

"You had to say it," Wesley murmured, cranking his crossbow string back with fervent effort as the Miquot sprouted several nasty blades along its arm and tore one off to fling at them—

—*missing?*

"He missed!" Gunn said in surprise, setting another bolt into place. *Aim and fire*—

"So I noticed." Wesley released another shot; it buried itself in the Miquot's throat, which actually staggered the demon. The joggers weren't slow to take advantage of their reprieve . . . they grabbed each other's hands, cast Wesley and Gunn identical, terrified looks, cast the Miquot an even more terrified look, and ran.

The Miquot yanked Gunn's arrow from its arm and threw it to the ground, heading for both Gunn and Wesley even as they released a simultaneous third salvo.

"Pincushion," Gunn said, not hesitating as he reached for another bolt. "Not doing much good."

"None of this makes any sense," Wesley admitted,

backing up several steps as the Miquot's reorienta-tion became a charge. "How those women survived even a moment—"

Gunn backpedaled, gave up on the crossbow—no way to get it cocked in time—and fell back to its convenient secondary function as the Miquot came within strides of them and turned for Gunn's own personal self. He met the demon head-on and bashed it across the head. More wood splintered an instant later as Wesley did the same from behind.

The demon turned on Wesley, beyond fury, beyond thought, leaking nasty Miquot blood from every wound. Wesley made a noise of profound surprise. "That shouldn't have worked!" he cried, stumbling back over the weapons bag with just enough time to pick the whole thing up and fling it at the demon. The Miquot knocked it away and leaped on Wesley.

Great. No crossbow, no weapons bag, berserker Miquot who didn't seem to know enough to grab his own homemade knives—

Gunn gave a feral grin. He jumped the Miquot, wrapped himself around the demon—who had wrapped himself around Wesley. All three of them crashed to the ground. With a fierce tug, Gunn freed one of the Miquot's arm-knives and plunged it into the demon. A couple of times, just for good measure . . .

As Wesley struggled free, the demon gave a grunt and collapsed.

Slowly, Gunn and Wesley climbed to their feet, checking themselves for serious injury even as they eyed the Miquot. The muscled, trained, excessively strong, perfectly intelligent Miquot who had, in essence, just stupided itself to death.

Gunn gave a little shake of his head; Wesley did the same. Together, they said, "This just isn't right."

And it wasn't.

Angel walked the boy to the sewer exit closest to his home and headed back for the Hyperion. Cordelia didn't emerge from hiding, leaving Angel free to worry about the toll of the visions on Cordelia and to dwell on his annoyance at having gotten nowhere with the hunt for his fake self—not to mention resisting the ever-present pressure of grim emotion.

Finally Wes and Gunn staggered in, the worse for wear. Slumping onto a roundchair, they eyed him. Compared with them, he was enviably intact.

"Saved a kid," Angel told them, all modesty.

"Saved the joggers," Gunn replied. "Where's Cordy?"

"Sleeping off the last vision, I think," Angel said. He sat in a neighboring roundchair and rubbed his hands over his face, unaccountably weary. Or maybe entirely with reason, given the unceasing battle against the feelings from within and without. Against Angelus.

Wesley frowned. His gray tattersall shirt was torn and spattered—L.L. Bean could probably expect a new order soon—and his usually starched posture looked more than a little wrinkled. At first glance, Gunn looked in better shape, but at second, it became evident the bounce was quite gone from his step and somehow he'd lost a shoe. Still obviously thinking about both boy and joggers, Wesley said, "So many in such a short time . . . it hardly ever happens."

"It's happening," Angel said flatly.

Gunn rested his head against the back of the roundchair. "At this rate we might as well just split up and patrol the streets tomorrow. Might save her some headaches if we're already on the spot."

Considering how close he'd been to the boy, Angel thought not. But he said nothing, having come to understand one thing about his formerly fellow man . . . people liked to take action. In fact, they liked to take it so much that sometimes they made up action to take.

From the second floor came Cordelia's anguished cry. They stiffened, exchanging glances, immediately recognizing the impact of another vision.

Wesley said, "Here we go again."

"I don't *know*," Cordelia sobbed, and at that moment the anger within Angel was entirely his own, fury at The Powers That Be who would allow such a burden to fall on her. Awkwardly, he nonetheless sat on the edge of the bed and put his arm around her. That she let him do it—that she actually leaned into the touch—did not strike him as a good sign.

From the grim tightness of Wesley's features, he was thinking much the same. Gunn paced at the doorway as though guarding it, his expression smoldering.

Monsters and demons might be easier to fight.

"It's okay, Cordy," Angel said, though he thought it wasn't. "Just tell us what you can."

"There's just too *much*—" She snatched a giant handful of tissues and sniffed loudly into them. "The Slith and the Miquot—"

They exchanged glances over her head.

"Cordelia," Wesley said gently, when no one else did, "we took care of them."

"Evidently not enough!" she snapped at him, a flash of temper that didn't last. "I'm sorry, it's just that these . . . these . . ."

"We know," Angel said. But they didn't. Not really.

"You don't remember anything else?" Gunn kept his spot by the door, easing just a little closer.

"I *wish*," she said miserably. "Miquot, definitely. And . . . people dying. I mean they must be. All that blood . . ." She curled away from Angel and pulled the pillow over her head.

Wesley caught Angel's eye, jerked his head toward the door. Feeling utterly conspicuous in conspiracy, Angel followed him out of the room. Fred slipped by them to take Angel's place on the edge of the bed, murmuring comforting words in a voice too soft to be heard.

"I don't remember ever seeing her like this," Wesley said, pitching his voice low. "There was that time she was hospitalized, but heaven forbid this should be another such episode—"

"I don't think it is," Angel said quickly, perhaps a little too quickly.

"That the time I was watching her for you?" Gunn said, and shook his head when Angel gave the slightest of nods. "I saw plenty of that. This isn't it. This is just . . . lots of things to have visions about."

"Except there's not enough detail there to *do* anything about whatever she's seen," Wesley said with some frustration.

Gunn gave a little laugh. "Look at us, Wesley. We couldn't do anything about it even if we *could*. I mean, I'm not saying I couldn't rise to the occasion—"

"Certainly not," Wesley agreed.

"—but we're all done in. And face it, if this keeps up, we're going to reach the point where we have to decide between saving a few people and figuring out what's going on."

"As for tonight . . . ," Wesley said thoughtfully, looking into the room.

Cordelia still hid under the pillow while Fred crooned some sort of lullaby; Angel doubted the others could hear it. He said, "There's an after-hours clinic not far from here. I'm taking her. They'll give her something strong."

"With any luck, strong enough to put her out for the night. And then tomorrow . . ."

"Let's just hope it doesn't start all over again," Gunn said.

Angel thought about getting Cordelia home after the clinic, and the reception they were likely to get from a certain overprotective ghost. "Someone better tell Phantom Dennis," he said, not bothering to hide his unease at the thought of a Dennis tantrum. He returned to the room to scoop Cordelia off the bed, pillow and all.

"Gunn can do that," Wesley said. "I'll drive you to the clinic."

"Me?" Gunn said. "Sad day when I find myself explaining things to dead people."

"*One* of you tell him," Angel said. "Or you're both going into her apartment ahead of me."

Fred made a *tsking* noise. "Phone," she said, trailing Angel out into the hall.

"He doesn't—," Gunn started, ready to dismiss

her—and then suddenly hesitating, understanding. "Bet he listens to her answering machine!" He and Wesley exchanged a look, then went for the stairs and the lobby phone.

Fred gave Angel one of her unexpectedly wise looks and said, "Unless, of course, she's got voice mail. Which I was going to add, but . . ."

"I'll send them in first, anyway," Angel said, and carried Cordelia down the hall.

The priests gathered not in the warrior's shrine, but along a rare stretch of nearly abandoned beach. They sat on a blanket watching the sun set, watching the waves roll in and spill themselves out on the sand, and feeling the pulsing power of the missing warrior's stone.

Khundarr said, "I've confirmed it. None of us can reach the stone or he who possesses it at his temporary dwelling. But the man never leaves the stone behind when he leaves that hotel. We have but to wait for him to emerge from his dwelling. Kaalesh is there now; shortly I'll join him."

The elder priest said, "I understood him to be protected outside the hotel as well."

Khundarr shrugged—for a Tuingas demon, more of a shoulder drop than a lift. "This is true. But it is still a more vulnerable situation. We'll assess the circumstances as necessary. We'll try to not harm anyone."

A fellow under-priest snorted indelicately through his long-nose and said, "To my mind, this human's behavior indicates he knows he has something that we want back. He does not act like an innocent."

"True," Khundarr said. "But the one who protects him may not have an understanding of the situation."

"Then he is a fool," said the elder. "How can he ignore what happens all around him? Even the *Slith* are affected. What happened at the produce market is only a hint of the disasters to come."

"It wasn't a *disaster*," someone observed, keeping a modest posture.

"It could have been!" the elder snapped. His intensely wrinkled skin had plumped somewhat in this fresh sea air, and some of his vigor seemed to have returned along with it. "I still haven't received a satisfactory report on just why it wasn't."

"With respect," Khundarr said. "There are so many of us in the human world, and so few of us with any real experience. Much of our effort is spent in remaining unnoticed. The rest is focused on reacquiring the stone. We are simply grateful that the Slith left the market before anyone was hurt. That he was goaded into such behavior should be a warning to us all . . . we *must* retrieve the warrior's stone."

"On that we are agreed," the elder said grudgingly. As if he had a choice. The demon-stone feedback loop was already fast spiraling to a point of overload . . . and once it reached that point, not only would L.A.'s demons go insane, the stone itself would become unstable. Soon enough, if any Tuingas, priest or not, so much as touched it . . .

Violent implosion.

The elderpriest brushed sand off his foot and said, "We owe you much for recovering the young one's raw deathstone with no incident. Not only is it in preparation for its shrine, but you left no clues for those who . . ." and here his face tightened in extreme distaste, for he'd seen the condition of the stone when Khundarr returned it.

Khundarr said soothingly, "I doubt those who had the stone understood the significance of the cleansing treatment they gave it." On the other nose, he also doubted that he'd left no clues for the people in that huge old hotel. The one had seen him, albeit in the darkness. And the hotel as a whole reeked of supernatural activity. The occupants might not have immediately understood the nature of the very private death rituals of a very private demon clan, but they were more equipped than most to figure it out. Not only that, but the young Tuingas wouldn't have died there in the first place had the hotel not had some connection to the warrior's stone.

It was a connection Khundarr intended to figure out.

CHAPTER SEVEN

The next evening, three demon hunters stood outside Baskin-Robbins, manfully pretending it wasn't just a little bit late in the season for after-dark ice-cream cones. Not that Angel would ever have ice cream under the beating sun again, but then he wasn't sure he'd ever had it that way in the first place. He pondered his memories, trying to identify the first ice cream. All he could remember was the ice cream he'd had with Buffy, that brief day he'd had in the sunlight. The one no one else would ever remember. "What kind did you get?" he asked Gunn, uncertain of the garish colors, and needing something to take his mind off the increasing throb of emotion in the night.

"Some Shrek thing," Gunn said, as if it hadn't been his choice at all. Nice try.

As often happened, Wesley's thoughts were off somewhere else entirely. "Cordelia said she thought the joggers and the Terminal Market thing were connected," he said, taking a quick lick around the edge of his ice-cream cone. His glasses sat a little askew on his nose, and his cheekbone was taking on a fine purple edge—both courtesy of an earlier minor demon encounter. But things had been quiet since then. "I think she's right."

Cordelia herself had spent the day in a haze, still groggy and so far blessedly free of visions; Wesley had checked the meds the clinic had given her the night before and suspected that their long half-life allowed them to interfere with any visions that might be lurking. Angel hoped they lasted a good long time.

"Connected *how?*" Gunn said. "Other than the fact that we're the good guys and we're kicking demon butt?"

"But it's not the kind of demon butt we'd ordinarily find ourselves kicking," Wesley said, adding a little feeble smile of acknowledgment to the two young women leaving the store as they each gave the trio an odd look. "Didn't mean to say that so loudly . . ."

"I don't think they heard you," Angel said. "I think they were looking at the ice cream all over your chin."

Wesley fumbled for a napkin. "You might have said—"

Gunn said flatly, "Demon butt is demon butt."

Repairs to his appearance complete, Wesley said, "Not necessarily. You know as well as I that many of these demon clans are highly intermixed with human blood. Some of them even pass for human."

Angel thought of Doyle, winced at a loss that still felt sharp. "Yes," he said. "Some of them do."

"And some of them are of little danger, anyway. Little more danger than your average human, that is."

"Your point being?" Gunn, still patently unconvinced, balled up his napkin and tossed it into a trash receptacle with absent pinpoint accuracy.

"*That's* who we've been fighting these past few days! The kind of demons we ordinarily wouldn't encounter."

A fleeting echo of his own earlier thoughts passed through Angel's mind . . . how the Slith demon might be feeling the same thing that he himself struggled with . . . how the normally mild creature would be less equipped to deal with such intensities. He didn't want to say it out loud, not if the result was the kind of distrustful looks he'd endured from his friends since they'd marginally accepted him back into the gang. More than marginal, now, but he had the feeling it wouldn't take much to change that.

Except one never knew what tidbit of information

would prove to be the key. *This* tidbit, maybe. Resigned to discussing it—*revealing* it—Angel opened his mouth—

"I don't buy it," Gunn said, gesturing with his Shrek cone. "What about the Miquot? Damned thing grows its own knives from its arms, Wes. Don't tell me it's the shy wallflower type."

"No . . . ," Wesley said slowly, and Gunn raised an eyebrow, one that meant *see?* Undeterred, Wesley said, "But its behavior was still entirely out of character."

"Unless those joggers were a lot more than they seemed," Angel agreed. *Another time.* He'd find another time to tell the others about the dreams. About how he'd had a hard time coming back from vamp-state the day before.

Maybe.

Or maybe he wouldn't have to. Maybe they'd sort this thing out without a *true confessions* scene.

Wesley shook his head, oblivious to Angel's inner dialogue. "A background check revealed nothing."

They both looked at him in surprise. He shrugged slightly. "I had time today. I was being thorough."

"You were being anal-retentive," Gunn said, but his voice had taken on a more thoughtful tone.

A trio of girls on skates zipped by, giggling as if by mutual accord. The ice-cream slurping manly men paused the conversation to watch.

"We ought to get back to the streets," Gunn said, still watching.

"I'd like to point out that we *are* on the street," Wesley said, also watching. Fumbling without looking, he threw his ice-cream-smeared paper napkin away.

"Good thing Cordelia's not here," Angel said, with less watching than the others, and more imagining of Cordelia's disdain. More distraction by . . . whatever-it-was.

"What?" Gunn snorted. "Like she doesn't do her share of ogling? She just uses her magazines."

"What is it about that?" Angel asked, thinking not of Cordelia at all—but of the false Angel. "Does she really admire those people, that life?"

Wesley turned to look at him with some surprise. "Not as much as she thinks she does, I imagine. Naturally that lifestyle has a certain allure to it . . . but when push comes to shove, she's got a good head on her shoulders."

"Yeah," Gunn said. "She knows what's important."

Angel said, "What?"

As one, they turned looks of suspicion on him.

"Hey," he said. "It's just a question. A fair question. What you admire in people . . . *who* you admire."

"Ah," Wesley said. "Having trouble with what she said about that fellow who's imitating you?"

"Don't go looking for any deep meaning," Angel said, which they all knew meant *yes*. "Just answer the question. Who do *you* admire?"

They looked at him a moment. Then Gunn said, "Lots of people. Like people from my neighborhood who work to make it better. Annie, for one. She makes some bad choices—like that whole Wolfram and Hart fund-raiser thing—but she has heart. She walks her talk."

Angel raised an eyebrow at Wesley, who said, "My turn, is it? All right then. Barney Clark."

Gunn said, "Who?"

"The first man to have an artificial heart," Wesley said. "He knew it wouldn't save him. But he was going to die, anyway, so he did it for all the people who would be helped by it, not for himself."

Angel considered them for a moment, while as if by unspoken agreement they left the Baskin-Robbins storefront and headed back to the dark corner where they'd stashed their weapons. Angel shook his head. "This fake me . . . it's just not right. He's either got the wrong guy, or he's imitating me for all the wrong reasons."

"So?" Gunn said easily. "You'll find him and you'll stop him. The end."

More understanding, Wesley said quietly, "This young man may know nothing of your history. He may simply admire what he sees today."

"Who I was and who I am . . . those aren't two separate things," Angel said.

"I know that," Wesley said, still quiet, still understanding. "But he may not."

Angel glanced at Gunn. "I guess I'll find him and I'll stop him. Then he'll know."

Behind a garbage bin, beside an alley squatter, they collected their weapons. Not things to carry on the street . . . not when the street was still full of light and people. They tipped the alley squatter for watching the weapons—well, mainly for not rushing out to sell them—and headed toward downtown. "Maybe we should split up," Wesley suggested, even as his phone rang.

He answered it, listened for a moment, and then moved the phone away from his mouth to murmur an aside to Gunn and Angel. "It's Cordelia," he said. "She's had another—I *am* listening, Cordelia. You're sure it was MacArthur Park—? *Near* the park. The post office?"

He muttered a few soothing words Angel could have heard if he'd tried; already they were headed back for the GTX. When he finally tucked his phone away, he shook his head. "This is taking quite a toll on her," he said. "Whatever's inspiring this rash of visions, we'd better figure it out fast."

"What're the goods on this one?" Gunn asked, casually hopping over the side of the convertible and into the backseat.

"She says it's the guy with the bowling ball bag—and another of our unidentified demons. Or rather, that it *will* be. I'm not sure how much time we have."

"We'll get there," Angel said grimly enough to draw a look from Wesley—but only until he accelerated away from the curb, leaving Gunn to whoop in a sarcastic-sounding tone and Wesley to clutch the door frame as he sank back into the seat. Down South Alvarado they went, until they hit Seventh and took a sharp turn, the outside wheels definitely light on the ground. A quick couple of blocks and they rolled into the empty parking lot near the post office, parking slantways across three spaces.

"Officer Friendly wouldn't approve," Gunn said sternly, jumping out of the car.

"Officer Friendly seems to be missing this party," Angel said, barely paying attention as he went into hunting mode—listening with the full scope of his hearing, fully attuned to the noises of the night. The ones that belonged, he ignored . . . and the ones that didn't . . .

. . . Like that harsh if distant scuff of shoe leather against asphalt . . .

"This way," he said, voice low, already moving. Heading between two close-set buildings, spilling out onto Bonnie Brae . . . he hesitated, heard a muffled word, and lit into full run, curving back into the next alley down and feeling himself go fang-face in the process. Not caring. Barging full speed between the two creatures scuffling in the alley and turning back on them with no plan at all—and not caring. Behind him—far behind him—Wesley shouted something. Something temperate, no doubt, something wise and restrained.

Not caring.

Just for once to feel again the unrestricted swell of strength and freedom and the power that was his. Uncontrolled . . . magnificent fury. Two beings were on the ground before him, each struggling to regain his feet. One a human, carrying a heavy leather bag . . . it should have meant something to him. The other not human, waving an extra appendage around as it attempted to regain its balance—and that should have meant something to him too.

It didn't.

He knew only that he wanted to kill them both . . . and that he could. *But . . .*

Heeding some tiny voice of sanity, he turned on the creature. Fellow demon. The thing roared something at him, met him in mid-charge; for a moment, they grappled like football players.

The creature's neck was thick and stumpy . . . well-muscled.

Angel broke it.

The human was nowhere to be seen. Angel took a step toward the back of the alley, casting his gaze along the roof tops. A scent on the breeze . . . familiar blood. He thought he saw a glimpse of dark, spiky hair, just visible as someone peered over the roof; he heard a definite swish of leather. A familiar noise to someone who so often wore a leather duster himself.

"Angel!"

That was Wesley . . . coming to a stop in the alley behind him. Annoyed, and about to demand an explanation.

Anger swelled—

No. Wesley was his friend. Gunn . . . Gunn didn't want to be his friend, but he was a colleague. Angel closed his eyes, fought to find his center— the eye of calm in his personal hurricane. That calm which tucked his demon aspects safely away once again, so he could turn and face Wesley and Gunn without triggering wary suspicion.

"What *happened?*" Wesley said, breathless from his futile attempt to keep up.

"Angel hogged all the fun, that's what happened," Gunn said, coming to a stop on the other side of Angel, looking up to see whatever it was that had held Angel's attention.

Wesley scanned the alley, found nothing, returned his frowning gaze to Angel. "What was that it said . . . er, roared?"

Angel shrugged. "Nothing in any language I speak," he said. "Does it matter?"

"One never knows." Wesley glanced at Gunn,

his frown turning to more of a puzzled expression as he sniffed the air. "Do you smell . . . it seems familiar . . ."

"Oh yeah," Angel said. "Watch where you step."

Gunn glanced down, jumping aside. "Hold on, isn't this—"

"The same substance I cleaned off the hotel floor just a few days ago," Wesley said dryly. "It would seem that whatever they are, they're still after the faux Angel's client—whoever *he* is. I expect he's around here somewhere. Or *was*."

"Faux Angel," Gunn snorted. "I like that."

Angel eased down the alley, scouring old asphalt and tufty weeds and broken glass for any small piece of something that might actually mean something. Faux Angel. *He* didn't like it at all. And he had to squelch annoyance at what he knew was coming next from Wesley, reminding himself once again that the feeling wasn't all coming from within.

It couldn't be. He couldn't handle it if this was all *him*—

"Was it necessary to kill it?" Wesley said. "It might have led us to our impersonator."

"*My* impersonator," Angel said. "It was a demon, Wesley. It was attacking someone. I didn't stop to ask why—I just stopped it. I can't help it they're so damn fragile."

"I rather doubt that they are," Wesley said,

packing a lot of meaning behind it: *You were out of control.* "And under the circumstances, I think it's more important than ever that we try to identify its language, and what it might have said. Especially since"—and he cast Angel another look in the darkness—"we had no chance to get another look at it."

Gunn stared off back down the alley. "How about we just take a look at that one?"

Hardly more than a dark lump in the night that blended against the deep shadows of the building, something moved.

"It's over near the remains of the first one," Wesley murmured—although when he took a step, the dark lump moved sharply, alert and wary.

"Checking out the demon goo," Gunn said. "I could circle back behind it—"

"It won't be here that long," Angel said shortly. It was, in fact, making its exit, a slinking retreat along the side of the building. He couldn't let that happen—it was the time for *answers.* He deftly appropriated the small but heavy war ax from Wesley's hand, hefted it—and even as Wesley cried a protest, flung it at the barely discernable figure.

There was a thunk—not metal sinking into flesh, but blunt weight bouncing off it. A hit, but he'd misjudged the distance, hadn't compensated with his grip so the weapon rotation would bring it blade first into its target. The demon shouted in pain . . . and ran.

Wesley turned on him, no longer restraining his anger. "Are you *trying* to turn every possible clue into goo? What on earth is the matter with you?"

"I was trying to stop him, not kill him," Angel said, emotion thrumming against his soul like the heartbeat he no longer had. Once released, it didn't ease . . . didn't ebb into the night as it should have. No respite here.

Gunn ran to where the demon had been, grabbing up the ax. "Doesn't look like you did *either*. I'll tell you this much, though—if this particular puddle of demon had one of those odd stone things, it doesn't have one anymore."

"That's what his companion was after?" Wesley said.

"If it had anything to be after at all—besides us," Angel said, and shrugged, so much more casual on the outside than on the in.

"Well, we can't *ask* him, can we?" Wesley said as they went to join Gunn. "We can't ask *either* of them."

Angel stopped, blocking Wesley's path. "Let it go, Wesley," he said softly. Dangerously.

Wesley met his gaze for that moment, searching it. Looking hard. Obviously shaken, but not letting it turn him away. Finally he lifted his chin somewhat, the smallest of acknowledgments . . . and no indication at all if he'd found what he'd been looking for.

More or less oblivious as he prowled around the entrance to the alley, Gunn said, "Fr'nnglekakggh. I think that's what he said. You think Lorne might recognize it?"

Angel said evenly—far too evenly, with too much effort to keep it that way—"Let's find out."

CHAPTER EIGHT

"Fr'nnglekakggh," Wesley said with evident concentration as he stood by the Caritas bar, fresh off their most recent encounter with the mystery demons. A nearly human bartender—Barbie doll proportions, long and luxurious red hair, skimpy costume, catfish feelers beside a lamprey mouth—slid behind Lorne to make change at the register.

"I think it was more like *fr'nnglekakkkh,"* Gunn said, spitting a little in the process and clearly distracted by the skimpy costume.

Angel listened with half his attention, uneasy in the crowded nightclub. In the background someone onstage warbled a song he hadn't yet been able to identify. Behind the songbird, customers spilled across the stage, taking what seating they could find.

Someone jostled him from behind, and he

whipped around just shy of fang-face, his glare enough of a warning for anyone.

"Lighten up, bub," said the hefty man who'd bumped him. He wore a mechanic's shirt with the name BIFF embroidered over the pocket and his belly stressing the buttons. The pale blue color played nicely off the lichen-like colors of his skin. "You won't impress any of *us* with that stuff." Then he looked over Angel's shoulder to where Gunn continued to argue pronunciation with Wesley while Lorne's increasing impatience manifested itself in a wandering gaze. "Is that . . ."

"Gunn," Angel said, a little bemused. "Works with me. Why?"

"Nothing. Nothing. You just hear stor—I mean, nothing. I'll just come back when it's not so crowded here." And the man made an overly casual if speedy about-face.

Huh. Not impressed by the vampire who was once Angelus, but one look at oblivious Gunn . . .

Of course, Gunn was human. Not restricted by the spell that kept demon violence out of Caritas. *That must be it.*

Definitely.

Behind him, Lorne finally spoke up in response to Wesley's and Gunn's hacking and spitting and general mangling of the demon word. Exasperation came through clearly in his voice. "Busy here, my oblivious little mood meter," he said. "In case you hadn't noticed. You want to settle on one word or the other? Because one of them means 'gimme' and the other means 'come light up my lair, perfume face,' and they're entirely different languages."

Angel turned to them, joining the conversation for the first time. "Gimme," he said. "That makes sense."

"Unless it was a girl demon with a thing for vampires," Gunn said, wincing a little at the notion. Or possibly at the music, for a new demon had taken the stage and was wobbling his way through "Billy, Don't Be a Hero." "And anyway, gimme *what?*"

Angel gave a quick shrug, a twitch-a-fly-off-the-shoulder movement. "I don't know. But it wanted something."

"That seemed clear enough," Wesley agreed. "Which language is it, Lorne?"

"The 'gimme'? Some Tuingas clan . . . maybe all of them." He put the finishing touches on several drinks in quick succession, and distributed them to customers waiting along the bar. "It's a widespread bunch. It's not like I could tell you even if I did have the time to think about it."

"You running a special or something?" Gunn asked, looking around the room with new interest . . . the gleam he got sometimes when he thought he saw someone he knew from the streets . . . possibly someone he'd tried to kill there.

"Keep your eyes to yourself," Lorne snapped at him. "They come in here to get away from their troubles, not find new ones."

"Exactly," Wesley said. "What's driving them here?"

"Same thing that keeps that little Slith fellow hanging around even now that I've turned him loose," Lorne said, mixing another drink with economical skill. "I'd charge him rent if he were any bigger, but he sleeps on top of the stage spot. Keeps him warm, he says. It's out of my way, so—"

"Fear," Angel said, his voice low. "Anger."

Baffled, Wesley said, *"Whose?"*

"Now *that*," said Lorne, "is the question. Isn't it?"

Angel looked at the puzzled expression on Wesley's face and the suspicion on Gunn's, and said simply, "It's in the air. If you're a demon, that is." He didn't elaborate on just what it felt like. Not yet. It wasn't as though he actually had any answers for them . . . only more questions.

Besides, he had things under control. Really.

He turned to Lorne. "These Tuingas," he said. "I've never heard of them as being one of the violent clans."

"Generally they're not," Lorne said, sprinkling flakes of something across the top of a murky drink and a huge martini glass and nodding with satisfaction when something came to the surface just long enough to suck the substance down. He handed the drink to his bar help; her catfish feelers quivered like Cordelia with an opportunity to schmooze with producers, but she put it on her tray and took it out to the floor customers. "But it's a huge clan, and a secretive one—they spend a lot of time in pocket dimensions, avoiding humanity altogether. Who's to say what would irritate them?"

"I think we can safely say we know someone who has," Wesley said. "If not just how he's done it."

Gunn crossed his arms across his Mickey Mouse T-shirt. "My vote? Next time we see that fellow, we forget about whatever other demons crop up in the vicinity and latch on to *him*. I'll bet we'd get some answers then."

Lorne paused in his work long enough to pin a sardonic red gaze on Gunn. "Well, Boy Wonder, while you're at it, see if you can find out just what's stirring up my customers. Not that I can't use the business after that little remodeling job, but this just isn't the sign of a happy community. And the seniors are going to get really cranky if tomorrow's Golden Oldies night is crowded out."

"We'll see what we can do," Wesley said. "But we've got to figure out what's up with this impersonator's client, so I can't promise much."

"That works out just fine," Lorne said, quite acerbically. "I'm not expecting much."

• • •

Gunn took a deep breath of the cool night air. He supposed most people would say it stank of exhaust and smog, especially on a fall night when the colder air sank into the city. Gunn himself found it refreshing.

Not refreshing enough to revive him to alertness—not at the end of a long few days with the wavering notes of the latest off-key Caritas performer still stuck in his head. Wesley didn't look any better off; he walked along with his glasses in his hands, frowning as he gently tried to bend them back into shape.

Only Angel seemed to be alert—but to judge by his expression, his quick attentiveness to noises that Gunn couldn't even hear, Angel was more than alert. He was on edge.

No kidding. As if that hadn't been obvious enough in the alley earlier this evening. And what was that casual comment in Caritas? *It's in the air.* Just what did that mean? If Angel knew something and one of the self-confident—okay, *overconfident* —new demon watch kids was hurt because of his silence . . .

Out loud, Gunn said, "What did you mean 'it's in the air'? What's in the air?"

"Quiet," Angel said, sharp but low.

Gunn gave him a mildly annoyed look. "Don't be hushing me, Fang-boy. Just answer the question."

Wesley put his glasses on, wiggling them into place and not looking pleased with the results.

"Lorne would have told us if he knew." Implying, of course, that Angel didn't really know either.

Angel turned on them, fangs flashing, ugly-face in full bloom. "I said, *be quie*—" But he broke off to whirl back around again, crouching slightly.

Pissed as he was, Gunn knew better than to ignore *that*—as did Wesley. They bumped up against each other, back-to-back, scanning the streets.

With a great clamor of yipping and whooping, a small pack of mixed demons barreled out of the nearest side street, hitting a streetlight without hesitation and bearing down on Gunn, Wesley, and Angel. For an instant Gunn wondered if their best chance was *break and run like hell,* but in the next he realized that the gang charged at such speed that they couldn't possibly stop in time for any true engagement. At his back, Wesley shifted uneasily and settled, as if racing through the same thoughts.

But Angel snarled softly and stepped out to meet the charge head-on, exchanging a flurry of blows. A spiked baseball bat clattered to the ground; a demon grunted and staggered aside to collapse—and then the rest of them charged right on by, licking out with a few cheap blows and then disappearing into the darkness.

"Ow, dammit," Gunn said, flexing a numbed wrist and frowning into the night.

"What was that—?" Wesley sounded dazed.

Gunn twisted around to check, and found him with fingers pressed to a small cut in his forehead.

Angel said grimly, "They're coming back," and stepped out to take point on the other side of the Gunn-Wesley formation. On that cue, the demon gang renewed their yippety battle cries and came rushing out of the darkness. Gunn scooped up the abandoned weapon and put it to his shoulder like a batter at the plate. He had an instant to watch as Angel clashed with the leaders, exchanging brutal blows, and then it was his turn. "Keep your eye on the ball," he muttered, and aimed appropriately.

Something screamed.

Then they were gone again—except this time there were bodies littered around the street, three of which lay at Angel's feet. Gunn found himself panting with the intensity of the brief exchange, and this time he didn't take his attention from Angel. Not when Angel was the one who could hear them coming.

But Angel straightened, human-faced again. He nudged a demon with his foot. Just an ordinary demon mutt from a whole gang of demon mutts. "This was their leader," he said. "I don't think—" He stopped short, lifting his head slightly to listen.

"Run?" Wesley suggested.

"We can beat their butts—," Gunn protested. They had half the gang's weapons scattered around them, after all.

Angel gave a sharp shake of his head. "Reinforcements," he said shortly.

They ran.

They pelted down the streets, mere blocks from the hotel, running flat out—and if they lost the demons along the way, Gunn wasn't about to stop just to make sure. Stumbling and wheezing, they burst into the hotel and slammed what was left of the doors behind them. Even Angel looked winded, leaning against the doors while Wesley bent over his knees and Gunn propped himself up on the stairwell.

"Lost them?" Wesley gasped, looking over at Angel without straightening.

"Not so much that as something else distracted them," Angel said, nonetheless peeking out the door.

Cordelia's head popped up over the back of the couch, tousle-haired and sleepy-faced. "What's going on?"

Wesley immediately straightened, Gunn slumped behind the stair railing, and Angel quickly assumed his most nonchalant face—unfortunately, always a clear giveaway. Sleepy or not, Cordelia narrowed her eyes at them.

"Nothing, why?" Angel said, and tried a little smile.

"Certainly, nothing," Wesley fumbled, not trying the smile.

"We sure weren't running our sissy little butts away from anything," Gunn said, and sprawled back against the steps with his arms spread wide.

"Whatever," Cordelia said, and disappeared back into the couch. "Can you just *not run* a little more quietly?"

But Gunn was no longer thinking of their close escape. He stared at the needs-paint ceiling and said, "How many people out there aren't running fast enough?"

Midday at the Hyperion, with the trusty Angel Investigations gang all . . .

Recovering.

Mostly recovering from the night before, when Wesley, Gunn, and Angel had gotten into the middle of a whatever it was on the way home from Caritas and then arrived at the Hyperion to find Cordelia sleeping in this very same couch, lost in the old K-O from a single vision.

None of them were quite themselves today.

Cordelia flipped a page in a magazine she wasn't really seeing, not even if it *did* involve someone shirtless and muscled. Her head ached like something bruised . . . bruised and yet still open for business, vulnerable to another pounding series of visions.

She very much dreaded there were more to come.

Another page. Ah, Tom Cruise. She sank further into the comfy overstuffed lobby couch between the stairs and the front desk, and prepared herself to be interested. More about the way he helped that woman after her car accident, and kept those boys from being crushed . . . hero material, all right.

Just like their Angel. At his good moments, anyway . . . and sometimes even when he struggled so hard with it that he made things difficult for all of them. She didn't get the big deal about this guy who was imitating him. Well, okay, so the guy was drawing customers that should have been theirs. And he would give them a bad rep if he mishandled cases. But that wasn't what had upset Angel . . . those were excuses. No, Angel just didn't like the idea that someone might imitate him at all.

That he might be worth imitating. The flattery part of it.

Possibly a little tough for a guy who went around carrying his various guilts like some sort of brooding cloak.

"Get over it, Angel," she muttered to herself.

Or perhaps not to herself after all.

The man had only been able to come in unnoticed because of her vision-battered state—or so she quickly decided. And he looked familiar. . . .

She did a quick mental inventory of the others— Wesley, scowling over vague references to Tuingas demons in his office and idly tapping the desk with his new chopsticks until she wanted to run in and wrench them away from him; Angel off in his room for a midday nap; Fred wherever she was hiding; and Gunn taking care of something in the neighborhood.

She and Wesley, basically, not that the man had noticed either of them yet.

And then she recognized him.

"Are you going to stick around this time?" she asked him, not bothering to hide the accusing tone in her voice. "Or are you just here to lure in another demon? Because let me tell you, it was so fun cleaning up after you the last time."

He whirled around, startled. But he recovered quickly enough, she had to give him that. He shifted his grip on that silly bowling ball bag and said, "That wasn't intentional."

"Worked out pretty well for you, though, didn't it?"

"I couldn't say," the man told her. "At least, not yet."

"Hmm." She closed the magazine, considering him from where she leaned comfortably into the corner of the couch. "Almost a conversation. That's progress, I suppose."

Wesley came to the open doorway of his office, hesitating there, his gaze going from Cordelia to the new arrival, as if trying to intuit their

127

conversation so far. From the look on his face, he probably had it pretty close. "Can we help you?"

Cordelia was glad to hear him use his frosty Englishman's voice . . . but in the end she knew, and she knew Wesley knew, that this could be a break for them. They couldn't quite afford to drive the man away.

"I'm looking for Angel," the man said, adjusting his poorly tailored jacket. It looked like a refugee from a 70s cop show, though the shirt beneath it was more disco in nature. "That is . . . I thought I *had* Angel, but now I'm not so sure. Truth is, I don't really care. I need protection. If you can give it to me, I'm yours."

"Something might be arranged," Wesley said. "But first we need some information."

"All you need to know is that I require protection and that it'll be over in a few days," the man said. "You don't need to know who I am or where I live or what I do."

"No," Wesley agreed, clearly surprising the man. "We don't. But we *do* need to know more about the man you've been with. The one who calls himself Angel . . . but isn't."

"Hey, he puts on a good show," said their possibly new client, totally unaware that a sleep-rumpled genuine Angel had come to the top of the stairs and was on his way down. Cordelia saw no reason to share. "He's got fangs, and I've seen his coffin. And he won't go out in daylight without that protective coat he's got."

"Without the *what?*" Angel said from the stairs, startling the guy entirely. Aside from his general glowering I'm-awake-and-it's-daytime demeanor, he'd come down barefooted and open-shirted and basically looked imposing enough to make any bowling ball guy think twice.

This bowling ball guy looked sheepish and said, "His coat. He said it was special, that it protected him."

"You know, you can buy fangs just about anywhere," Cordelia said, putting the magazine aside and pulling herself up to sit cross-legged on the couch. "This *is* Hollywood. Or, well, close enough."

On the stairs, Angel gave the slightest of grim smiles. Just enough to show his teeth . . . as fangface morphed to the surface and disappeared again, leaving the bowling ball guy blinking and uncertain.

Bemused, Wesley asked, "Did you say *coffin?*"

"I woke up in one of those once," Angel said. "Personally, I never saw any reason to go back."

"True," Cordelia informed the man. "No coffins here. He doesn't always make his bed, though."

"Hey," Angel said, offended. "You're messing with my impressive entrance."

The man glanced from one to another of them, his own expression beginning to grow a little desperate. "Look," he said. "Are you willing to help me or not? It's not that Ang—that the other fellow *isn't* so much as I think the job is bigger than one man can handle."

"That would seem evident from the way we keep cleaning up after both of you," Wesley said. "I don't suppose you'd care to tell us what you were doing near MacArthur Park last night. Or why you didn't stick around after we saved your life. A simple thank-you at that point would have sufficed."

"Why do you *think* I didn't stick around? I figured there were more on the way. If I could deal with these things I wouldn't have hired help in the first place."

"And just why is it that they want you so bad?" Cordelia said, getting to her feet to walk up to him, then around him. She crossed her arms and stood hipshot before him. Waiting. "What'd you do to get their attention?"

Angel said suddenly, *"Gimme."*

"That's right," Wesley said, straightening with suddenly focused interest.

"Possibly the clothes," Cordelia said, not sure what they were talking about with the whole *gimme* thing—for all she knew, they'd told her while she was in her fog. "*That* outfit would offend anyone with even the smallest amount of fashion sense."

One of the boarded-up hotel doors opened; the

new arrival stood poised in the opening, not quite ready to commit himself to a complete entrance. The backlighting made him into a dark silhouette, discernable only as a long coat with a head at the top and legs sticking out the bottom.

"By all means, come in," Wesley said.

"Yes," Cordelia said, although she wasn't nearly as blasé as she pretended. This faux Angel's client had been in at least one of her visions . . . and it suddenly occurred to her that between them, maybe he and the client could help resolve whatever had been causing the recent agonizing run of the things. "Come right in out of that nasty daylight."

She couldn't see his expression; his body language looked unconvinced. But he came in and let the door close—in its current crooked way—behind him.

For a moment they all just looked at one another.

Cordelia eyed the faux Angel in particular disbelief. *If there is such a thing as Fashion Police, we're all doomed.*

Okay, sometimes Angel's look got a bit monotonous—all that gray and black and subdued stuff, and if he ever broke loose and went for something in a jewel tone, it never really worked. But at least he didn't wear pants that were too short along with bulky white sneakers. His spiked brush-up hair had a natural look—and well it might, considering he could hardly use a mirror to style it and until recently hadn't even seemed to be aware of the look at all. The faux Angel's hair appeared hard and spiky and could probably have been used as a weapon if he ever failed to run from a fight. His poorly fitted black duster swept the ground and drooped from his shoulders. His glasses were hopelessly without style. And he'd cinched his belt up high. Too high. Angel's expression hit high disbelief as he gave the new arrival the once-over, then a twice-over, then looked down at himself as if to double-check that he didn't, indeed, look like this imitation.

"Ugh," Cordelia murmured, voicing everyone's thoughts. "Wedgie country."

She wasn't sure *he* thought any better of them. Except . . .

Except for Angel. The faux Angel's expression as he took in the real vampire—in his rumpled state looking more menacing than skinny Faux Angel could hope even on his most bulked-up day— flickered between respect and a hint of chagrin. But in the end he must have decided to bluff it out, for he straightened his narrow shoulders and set his weak jaw. "My client has all the protection he needs from me," he said, and looked at the man. "Let's go."

"Ohh, I don't think so," Angel said, even as Wesley slipped behind Faux Angel, blocking the exit.

"There's this small matter of using my name. Sure, go ahead and pretend you're a vampire. Plenty of people do, even the ones who don't really believe we exist. But the name thing? *No.*"

"To be honest," Cordelia said, using her most helpful voice, "you really can't pull it off. I mean, sure, you have the basic black thing down, but the overall look . . . that's not brooding. That's just plain sullen."

"That's not the point," Faux Angel said, sounding a little desperate. "I've been hired to protect this man, and I can do it. I've *been* doing it."

"Actually, to a large extent, *we've* been doing it," Wesley said, still blocking the doors. "And as long as we're involved—rather involuntarily, so far, I might add—I think you owe us an explanation."

"Or maybe he could just clean up the lobby the next time it gets gooed," Cordelia suggested.

"Or maybe," Angel said, coming down to the foot of the stairs and causing Faux Angel and his client both to back away a few steps, "maybe he should quit using my name, find another closet full of clothes, and go back to whatever real-life job he has. Before someone"—and he took a step closer to the men, his expression suddenly the one that always made Cordelia uneasy, the one where she was never sure if he meant the threat that lurked behind his eyes or if he was just really, really good at bluffing—"gets *hurt.*"

For an instant, Faux Angel looked baffled, as if this wasn't the way Angel was supposed to react to him—and in that moment he deflated, looking not remotely like Angel at all, but just a pathetic young man dressed in poorly fitting black. But then he seemed to draw an odd inspiration from Angel's anger . . . imitating on the fly, Cordelia realized with a numb surprise. Turning his expression into a pale version of Angel's. She felt an instant of skittering panic, realizing that Faux Angel was so far from having a clue and that the real Angel was so close to stepping over the line—

The doors burst open. Plywood cracked; the precariously surviving hinges gave way. Wesley went flying, his expression pure astonishment.

One of the Tuingas demons hesitated there, scanning the lobby—and then went straight for Faux Angel's client.

Not *again!*

And Cordelia couldn't believe it: Faux Angel looked like he might actually try to put up a fight. She bolted across the lobby to the weapons cabinet, grabbing the first things she could get her hands on—a small spiked morning star, a short main gauche—and flung herself back to the fight even as Angel grabbed the demon's attention from behind. The morning star went to Wes simply because he was on the floor and she couldn't imagine throwing it; Angel plucked the main gauche out of the air.

And then Cordelia had a second thought. "Don't kill it!" she cried. "Whatever you do, *don't turn it into goo!*" And then, realizing that Faux Angel had grabbed his client and had headed for the courtyard exit doors, she shouted, "Hey! Get back here! You little coward—you owe us a door! *Two* doors!"

But Faux Angel never paused. And when she turned back to the fight, Cordelia saw there was no longer any fight at all. Instead, there was a wary standoff. Wesley hadn't yet made it to his feet; he paused, crouching, on the way up. Angel stood back a step, the short blade ready . . . but hesitating. The demon itself had backed up to the broken doors, watching Faux Angel's escape. Just as she remembered from their first encounter, aside from the nasty and fresh-looking wound on its chest. Otherwise the same, big and bulky and basically humanoid, if only it'd had a neck to speak of . . . or if that . . . *thing* . . . hadn't been sprouting from its upper throat, currently coiled protectively around its neck, the tip glistening and flaring with each breath—

"Is that a *nose?*" she blurted.

The demon looked at them and snarled something short, sweet, and distinct that had Wesley diving for a piece of paper even as the thing turned on its flat, scaly heel and left, finishing off the right-hand door entirely on its way out.

In the wake of it all came silence, filled only by the slight creak of the door as it swung slightly on its one remaining hinge . . . and then let go, slowly easing its way to the floor.

"So!" Cordelia said. She thought she saw Fred lurking around the top of the stairs, investigating the noise—but decided to leave her secure in her lurkage. "What have we learned from this little encounter?"

"Fghlztt," Wesley muttered to himself, scribbling on the back of a take-out menu, his desk the floor. "Or was it *Fghaluzzt?*"

"We know that guy isn't anything like me," Angel said.

"We know I can check under Tuingas clan demons with prehensile noses," Cordelia said.

Fred's quiet voice said, "It's more what you *don't* know, don't you think?"

No one looked startled; like Cordelia, they must have noticed her right away, but didn't draw attention to her arrival. Aside from Wesley's mumbling, scribbling, scratching out, and rescribbling, no one made any immediate response either.

Fred inched down a step. "You don't know why that man tries to look and act like Angel. You don't know why the Tuingas demon wants the man in the ugly clothes. You don't know why the man in the ugly clothes would stick with the fake Angel instead of sticking with the real thing when he found it. You don't know why the demons turn to goo. You don't know why something broke in here and took the only part of the dead Tuingas that *didn't* turn to goo. And you still don't know why all the demons around here are causing such a fuss."

By then they were all staring at her, and her voice faded away. Much more tentatively, she said, "Maybe I missed something? Maybe there are more . . ."

"Oh, it sounds to me like you've hit all the highlights," Wesley said, sitting cross-legged on the floor with his notes. "The final question is, which, *we don't know* do we try to handle first?"

"There's more than one of us," Cordelia said, and slanted a look at Angel. "Most of us are even dressed."

He looked down at himself, plucking at his shirt. "What? Six buttons and I'm dressed. Ready to go. Rah-rah demon hunter."

"Puh-lease," Cordelia said. "I was a cheerleader, remember? You couldn't pull off a cheer if your unlife depended on it."

Wesley rolled his pen slowly between his palms as he stared thoughtfully at his scribblings. "I should do my best to decipher this—it looked to me like the creature was making a real attempt to communicate."

"Lorne might be helpful," Cordelia suggested. "I could—"

"Stay here," Angel said. "You're not in any shape to be out in whatever's going down."

"Oh, and thank you for noticing so loudly." She scowled at him, suddenly feeling every bit of all those accumulated visions. "I'll *call* Lorne." Or pore over the identification books. Now that she knew—or at least *suspected*—that the demon's mystery appendage was a nose, maybe she could pin down just which variety of Tuingas they were dealing with. Maybe there would be some little tidbit that would help make all this . . . make sense.

"And I'll—" Angel glanced at the open doorway and the sunlight streaming into the hotel. He'd done the sewer circuit already. *Time to hit the Internet?* "I'll hang around inside doing something very important until I can hit the streets."

"Maybe seeing about getting those doors fixed," Cordelia said, and went over to practice the words Wesley had written down until she thought she could do a half-decent job of pronouncing them.

But Lorne didn't want to talk about Tuingas words that had been spat in anger. "Honeychild," he said to her in his perfect mix of air-kissing and actual sincerity, "to judge by the last phrase your rogue demon hunter muttered at me, I haven't a chance in whatever hell you want me to swear by of figuring it out. I'm more interested in what you people have been up to. Do you know I couldn't even close last night? I could lose my license, not to mention too much sleep. Speaking of which, that's what's happening here now. They stayed awake all night, and now they're draped all over the club, snoring away. It's a real mess. You tell your boys that I'm *this close* to heading for that pitcher."

"But . . . ," Cordelia said, trying to imagine wall-to-wall club patrons, slumped in chairs, leaning on one another, faces on the tables. She sat at her desk, idly scrolling through the Dailynews.com Web site's headline page. *"Why?"*

"That's the sixty-four-zillion-dollar question, isn't it? That's what *you're* supposed to find out, doll. Whatever's going on out there has gotten them seeking safe haven in here. Not too many of those around this city." In the background, she heard water running. Significant water, splashing into a significant container.

She very much suspected he was running a bubble bath.

"Can't *you* tell what's got them scared?" she asked. "You're Mister Empathy Demon and all."

"Cordelia, sweetie," he said, then briefly hesitated, a moment during which she heard water splashing. "That's only if they're singing. As it happens, I've cut the power to the stage equipment. There's only so much one fella can take—you know what I mean? Even now I can feel them out there.

Most of them are having bad dreams. They're all angry at something . . . and I'm not sure any of them know why. Brrr!" he made an exaggerated shuddering noise.

"What?" she said intently, taking her hand off the computer mouse. "Did you feel something clueful—?"

"Need more hot water," he said, distracted. "Tell you what. Give me a little music. If *you've* got any clues lurking around in there, maybe they'll jump out at me."

"Since I'm Vision Girl and all, you mean," Cordelia said, not quite bitter. As much as they tore her up, they served a purpose. And usually that was okay; usually there was a balance. Usually they didn't come in batches that left her such a mess that she'd even cancelled a reading.

"Cordelia . . . *music,* honey." He must have shifted impatiently; she heard the gentle lap of water.

Music. Cordelia glanced at Angel—lurking by Wesley, his shirt buttoned, his breakfast blood in hand, clearly driving Wesley mad—and gave Lorne the wordless theme to the old Batman TV series. "*Da*-na-*na*-na-na-na—"

"Stop!" Lorne shouted, literally shouted. "Hang up!"

Cordelia removed the phone from her ear, giving it a frown. "But—"

She heard the distinct click as he broke the connection.

And then another kind of connection clicked in, the kind that ripped through her head and left scant clues in its wake. "No!" she said. "Nonononono*no!*" Enough already!

It came on, anyway.

CHAPTER NINE

"A whole flock of Slith?"

Angel stood by the front desk, behind which Fred was ministering to Cordelia, offering her water and . . . left-over sushi?

No doubt the only things in the fridge right now. Other than blood, of course.

"I don't think they're called flocks," Wesley said. "In fact, they gather in numbers so rarely, I'm not sure anyone *has* a name for what they form." He glanced at his watch and then out the office doors, where the sunlight had paled. "We should call Gunn. It sounded like it would go down in MacArthur—busy place lately, isn't it? And isn't he training a neighborhood watch group this evening?"

"Something like that," Angel said, feeling unhappier about it by the moment. "Never mind calling. Let's go. We'll call on the way."

"It's still—"

"I'll ride in the back, under the blanket," Angel interrupted him. "Let's *go*."

So close!

And yet not nearly close enough.

Kaalesh was dead, for nothing. Killed in a narrow L.A. alley as Khundarr's team attempt to retrieve the warrior's stone.

At least his deathstone was where it belonged, in a pocket dimension shrine.

Not here in the human world, ripping into the minds of demons benign and not so benign, building power into a feedback loop that not even the most mild of creatures could ignore. Stone to demons and back to stone again, which absorbed the amplified feelings and broadcast them yet again. . . .

Eventually the stone would lose stability. Eventually, so would the demons.

Khundarr, too, could feel it beat against him . . . but his priestly protections let him feel it from afar, feel it without taking it into himself.

Unlike the wound the vampire had dealt him the night before. Holy Rhinitis, that still stung.

The disposition of the people based in the old Hyperion Hotel still eluded Khundarr. They'd killed his fellow priests . . . and yet tonight, upon recognizing him and upon seeing his own intent to quit the fight, they had not pressed him. They protected he who possessed the stone . . . with no apparent awareness of its existence. They'd never glanced toward it or made any special move to save it . . . they merely reacted the way any Tuingas demon might react were his home invaded and his fellow clan members threatened.

And yet they of anyone in this city seemed to have the wherewithal to figure things out. They had artifacts that suggested a certain scholarship of demon life. They had a vampire among them, one who should be able to feel the effects of the warrior's stone—and to judge by his behavior the night before, certainly had not gone untouched by the stone's emanations, as much as he seemed to fight the results. Odd. Most vampires embraced such experiences.

If only those humans would listen to him . . . he'd told them quite plainly what he wanted. If only they'd *question* this man they protected. If only they'd see that the city was in a dangerous turmoil, and that soon . . . there would be no saving any of the humans here.

So close.

And not nearly close enough.

Angel hated riding in the back.

The blanket never felt like enough protection, but it nonetheless kept him from seeing where they were, and when he should brace for a red light—or, more often, for a careless driver switching lanes in front of them.

"Is it dusk yet?" he asked.

"Not in the sixty seconds since you last asked that question, no," Wesley said through obviously gritted teeth as the car idled in traffic.

It was stifling under the blanket even if he didn't need to do the breathing thing, and thick wool was the only thing he'd found that would really block the light but it was scratchy; made him itch. Surely it would be safe enough just to peer out as the car accelerated into an intersection and turned. *Surely* . . .

"Is it dus—"

"Yes!" Wesley snapped. "Yes, it's totally and completely safe even though only moments have passed. By all means, throw the blanket off and turn your face to the sky!"

A long silence filled the space between them.

"That's not fair," Angel told him, giving the blanket a baleful stare at the spot beyond which Wesley sat. "I don't think it would have been so funny if I'd burst into flame, now, do you?"

A very heavy sigh came in response. The car made a few more turns, cornering gently; the smell of newly mown grass filtered in through the blanket while Angel contemplated the significance of failing to raise Gunn on his cell phone. As Cordelia would have quickly pointed out, it could mean only that Angel hadn't dialed it correctly. Hard enough to use the things under normal conditions . . . even harder, huddled under a blanket in a moving car. Finally Wesley said, "It's safe. And we're almost there."

Angel hesitated only a moment—*no, he's not kidding this time*—and threw the blanket back as Wesley pulled in against the curb. As Wesley yanked the keys from the ignition and reached across the front seat to gather his gear—all crinkly in his rain suit—Angel put a hand out, a silencing gesture. The only way to be silent was to be still . . . so Wesley froze.

In the distance they heard what could have been the noise generated by a late soccer game.

Or not.

"Let's go," Angel said, and leaped out of the car. He'd brought the main gauche—handy as it had been—but in light of what had happened at Terminal Market, also a crossbow with plenty of bolts.

Wesley was armed likewise, and covered from ankle to neck with an outdoorsman's rain suit, his motorcycle helmet under his arm. "Gore-Tex," he'd said. "It breathes."

"Breathing is overrated," Angel had observed. But now he thought the rain suit looked easier to move in than his duster, which, zipped for protection, suddenly seemed a little restrictive.

Better than a hidden spitball in his clothes. They'd have to do a spitball inspection after this one regardless. Maybe they could even have a party.

It was a dark thought, matching the sudden change of his mood, the emotions that seemed to build with the night. *Not again . . .*

They ran into the park and followed the curves of Wilshire Boulevard, which split the park more or less in two—the lake on one side, pavilions and open space on the other, trees scattered all around.

"Of *course*," Wesley said, panting and gesturing at the park with his crossbow. "Slith like the water. But still, it makes no sense—"

"There!" Angel interrupted, pointing toward the northeast area of the park. A white-pillared pavilion, a flurry of activity. Dark blobs, running back and forth, crouching . . . cringing. Human in movement, if not in shape. The Slith were harder to spot in the growing dusk.

They angled in from the side, hunting for a crossfire position—but the pavilion faced a triangle full of trees, giving widespread and copious cover to the Slith. As Angel and Wes grew closer they heard Gunn urging the teens to take cover, and it was then that Angel understood the dark blobby nature of their appearance.

They all wore black plastic garbage bags.

Gunn was the biggest, tallest garbage bag among them, and the first to spot Angel and Wesley. "It's about time!" he called, grabbing the arm of a young man who seemed determined to charge off into the trees to stomp some Slith. Half of the teens seemed to be of the same mind, and the other half cowered against the pavilion. One of them jumped up, shouting in alarm and flapping his garbage bag to dislodge what must have been a spitball.

So much for sneaking in unseen. Not that they'd had much chance of that in the first place. They hesitated just to the side of the pavilion, with one good tree between themselves and the as of yet unseen Slith—although there was plenty of evidence that they were here. Spitballs on the ground, the repeated *poot* of another blowgun in use, scuffling movement back the trees.

"What did you *do?*" Wesley said with some exasperation, hesitating at the edge of the field of fire. By then, all the teens were watching them; some waited for them to save the day, but most seemed barely under Gunn's control, ready to do their own fighting in spite of the odds.

"Do?" Gunn repeated, offended. "*Do?* I thought fast, that's what I did! There we were, the neighborhood watch, out cleaning up the park—you know, good deeds, bonding, getting a clean park out of it on top of that?—and these things came

148

down on us. I got 'em gathered and covered up, that's what I *did*."

"What did you do to the *Slith*, that's what I want to know," Wesley said, persisting. "This just isn't like them."

"You'd better check your reality meter, English, because as far as I can see, this *is* like them. You gonna help us or not?"

Behind him, another of the teens jumped up, panicked, hitting at her garbage bag poncho while her friend tried to stop her. "Don't, you'll *touch* it!" the second girl said, grabbing at the hands of the first. "Just stay low!"

"Do as she says," Gunn snapped. "We'll deal with this."

Anytime now. Angel moved restlessly in the faltering light, cocking and loading his crossbow . . . and aware that whatever had driven the Slith to such fervor was also driving at his own senses.

"This just isn't right." Wesley declared, looking at the trees that hid the enraged Slith. He jammed his motorcycle helmet on, his face covered by the visor and his hands jammed in his pockets. With the rain suit zipped up tight against his throat, he was spitball-proof from head to toe. He stepped out between the trees and the pavilion and said more loudly, *"This isn't right."*

Not right that the whole park should reek of anger, emotions none of the humans seemed the least bit aware of. Emotions that Angel would begin to believe came from within if he hadn't had the evidence of the Slith before him. Meek Slith, retiring Slith, never-gather-in-a-group Slith . . .

Emotions that left him torn enough, uncertain enough, that he couldn't bring himself to confess them to the others. Not when they'd already had quite enough of that.

Wesley called, "We know something's bothering you—driving you to behave this way. We don't want to see you hurt. Please, leave these people alone and go back to your, er . . . homes."

No response.

Or was there? Hard to tell in this light, even for a vampire's eyes . . . but had the spitballs stopped?

Some deep part of Angel didn't want it to be so. Some deep part of him wanted to wade into those Slith demons and take them apart at the seams. Never mind the crossbow—just straight to the source. Bashing Slith against trees, against one another, their little stick legs breaking—

Stop it. He closed his eyes, took what would have been a deep breath.

"There, you see?" Gunn was telling the kids. "No big deal. Wesley's gonna talk them to death. And if anyone can do it . . ."

Wesley said to the silent trees, "We don't know what's going on, but I promise you, we're trying to find out. We're trying to make it better. If you'll only go back to your homes and stay there until we have a chance . . ."

For a long moment, no one moved. No one said anything. It was just Wesley, standing out in the open in his rain suit and motorcycle helmet. No scuffing, no flying spitballs, no puff of a blowgun in use. The Slith, decisively retiring in nature, probably knew as well as Wesley that this group melee was far from the norm.

Gunn said decisively, "Sinthea, Tyree—you two are in charge. The rest of you *aren't,* so don't try to be. It's time for a good strategic retreat, and you're gonna take it."

"Naw, Gunn, we want to take *care* of these things," one of the young men said.

"They don't need taking care of. They're angry, we're on their turf, and it's time to leave. Unless you got some nice armpit poison of your own to pass around?"

"He's got *that,* all right," one of the girls mumbled, and they all gave a nervous laugh.

Wesley pulled off his helmet and faced the pavilion, taking a few steps closer to it. From the trees, mostly silence. A little rustle. Maybe they'd actually been shocked into halting their barrage. As Wesley kept saying, it wasn't in their nature.

But then, only Angel knew just what they'd been feeling.

"Is everyone all right?" Wesley asked. "No one got hit in all the confusion?" He glanced at the ground, which was littered with little slimy paper balls. "It's a good thing that poison degrades so quickly, or we'd be here all night picking these things up."

"The little Muppets weren't really close enough to hit anything except by chance," Gunn said. "I think most of it landed right about where you're standing."

"What if it hadn't?" The girl named Sinthea stood in front of the others, armed with a sort of sullen bravery. "What if one of those things had hit us? And I don't even wanna *know* if they're living in the reservoir."

Wesley said dryly to Gunn, "I take it you've been training them for another sort of neighborhood watch than is usually meant."

Gunn gave a one-shouldered shrug. "What do you think?"

"Only in L.A., that's what I think," Wesley said. He turned to Sinthea. "The poison is a neurotoxin, and it acts quickly. It interferes with the body's functions and causes convulsions, a disruption of breathing and heartbeat, and can in some cases cause death." He tipped his head to regard her a moment, and then admitted, "In most cases, actually."

Sinthea said to Gunn, "He's the one who reads, right?"

More gently than Angel expected, Gunn said, "We *all* read. But Wesley does most of the research. I wouldn't have known we needed protection from the spitballs without it."

Althea looked back at the bushes as if considering the Slith and the danger they'd been, and then gave a decisive nod. "I'll think about it," she said, and turned back to the other teens, gathering them up like a shepherd.

"What—?" Wesley asked.

"Been trying to convince them to take all the advantages we can get. That means reading up on some of these things instead of just coming out and being tough."

"Ah," Wesley said, with the slightest of smiles—looking touched, actually.

Angel didn't care. Angel was reeling in being set up for a good fight and not getting it, and in the reverberations of emotion all around him, the emotion-that-wasn't-his . . . but had become his. The Slith, too, had been dealing with that; something within him still refused to believe they'd been talked down so easily. Something in him didn't *want* them to have been talked down so easily.

Or maybe Wesley's outfit had simply amused them out of their snit.

He said, "This is more than just a couple of strange incidents. This is . . ." *fury and the need to attack and fight back and revenge* and Wesley giving him a strange look . . . "I mean, we need to *do* something before something happens that we can't stop in time."

Gunn gave him a flat stare. "You *think?*"

Attack and fight back and—Angel felt the change come over him, couldn't stop it. He didn't *want* to stop it. In that instant, he didn't even try. He let it in, let the rage fill him . . . he turned on Gunn with all the frustration and roiling emotions that echoed around the park with no one but him to lodge in. He turned with his speed and his power and saw the astonished flash of understanding on Gunn's face just at the same time he saw a single remaining Slith crouch by the closest tree and raise a blowgun to its broad mouth. And he launched himself at Gunn, reaching, reaching . . .

. . . reaching . . .

. . . and snatched the little missile out of the air just before it landed on the skin of Gunn's neck.

The landing was nothing of power or anger or grace. The landing was a belly flop that rattled him even with no breath to lose.

"Angel!" Wesley said, somehow managing to make it sound like a questioning demand instead of just a demand. Angel, still stretched his full length upon the ground, didn't fail to notice where Wesley's loaded crossbow pointed. Neither did the teens exclaiming in the background.

The Slith scampered away into the night,

leaving his blowgun at the base of the tree and his maniac giggle lingering on the air.

Eyes on the crossbow, Angel opened his hand so Wesley could see the spitball, waiting for Wesley's quiet sigh of relief before he relaxed entirely himself.

"Gee," Gunn said from directly behind him. "For a moment there I thought you'd really turned on me. I mean, for a *moment*—but no, you were just using those demon reflexes of yours to save my life, weren't you?"

Angel heard the dark sarcasm behind the words; he didn't rise to them. He didn't have anything to say to them. So he said simply, "Yeah. That was it." Then he looked at the spitball, and at the sudden unbidden twitch of his fingers, and asked Wesley in his most casual voice, "So, how bad can it be?"

Wesley lowered the crossbow entirely, coming to crouch by Angel. He gave the spitball a somber look—as if he could discover some crucial fact by looking at it more closely—and used the crossbow tip to nudge it out of Angel's hand. He ground it into the dirt with his toe, and then said with a certain amount of false cheer, "Well, on the one hand, it's not on that short list of things that will kill you."

"And?" Angel said through slightly gritted teeth, watching the twitch move up his arm.

Absolutely no comfort at all, Wesley said, "On the other, you might wish that it had."

"Grea—" *Great.* But he never finished the word, for his head snapped back and his spine whipped into an arch so tight, it cracked. Blood from his bitten tongue coated his mouth and lips while pain scribed lightning across his brain. *Great.* Strong hands took his head, kept it from beating against the ground. Words reached his ears, garbled and meaningless and fading.

Wracked with pain, his own body tearing itself apart, Angel's last thought was relief. For that moment, the pounding anger lifted. For that moment, he knew again what was *him* and what was *other.*

For that moment, he was free.

He choked on a laugh, and the darkness overtook him.

"I'm telling you, he *laughed,*" Gunn insisted. His voice reached Angel's ears through a filter of muffled distortion.

"I rather doubt that," Wesley said, also sounding as if he were speaking through a glass of water. "Even if he'd wanted to, which I can't imagine, he was hardly capable."

"Oh, really? And how capable was he of attacking me? Or do you *rather doubt* that, too?" When he wanted to, Gunn could really put a British spin on his words.

Numb as he was, Angel felt a familiar lump in the mattress beneath him and knew he was back at the Hyperion Hotel, in his very own room. To judge from the smell, someone was thoughtful enough to have a glass of blood nearby. Probably Cordelia. He'd have to tell her thank you, just as soon as he could open his eyes and open his mouth and the remnants of Slith poison weren't coursing pain through his veins. Old blood coated his mouth . . . his own, and it tasted terrible. But his bitten tongue was already healing; he thought he might have the feeling back in his toes.

A wave of warning flushed through his body; every muscle clenched tight in spasm. He kicked somebody. Tighter . . . *tighter* . . . he thought his back might break . . . muscles screaming . . . *release*.

"God!" Cordelia said, tears quite audible on the edge of her voice. "How long is this going to go on?"

"I don't have any information on that," Wesley admitted, not sounding terribly concerned. "People don't generally last this long. But it seems to me the spasms are easing. We do know it won't kill him."

Cordelia sat on the bed; she'd probably been the one he kicked off in the first place. "Oh, and because we know it won't kill him, it doesn't matter that he's going through this?"

As muzzy as his thoughts were, Angel pretty much expected the silent response. He knew

Gunn was thinking about the moment Angel had turned vamp on him. He knew Wesley had seen it too.

In utter disgust, Cordelia said, "Men are such pigs."

Gently, Wesley said, "I'm afraid we also have other things on our mind. Important things."

With reluctance, Cordelia said, "Because you think he was going after Gunn." She shifted on the bed. "I wish I hadn't just said that."

Gunn's voice didn't have any of her reluctance, just a hard edge of anger. "I *know* it."

"Gunn, he *saved* you."

Entirely unconvinced, Gunn said, "He came for me. He just changed his mind along the way. Got distracted, maybe."

Definitely, Angel was regaining control of his toes. Not that they'd do him any real good in a fight, but it was a start. And probably he could even have said something, anything, to let them know he was awake. Or getting that way, anyway.

But he didn't. He listened.

Cordelia said slowly, "It's true . . . he's not right. He hasn't *been* right. It's more than just this faux Angel thing. Whatever's going on with these other demons . . . I think he's part of it. It's getting to him, too."

"Then we'd better *stop* whatever's going on. Before it's too late, if you get my drift," Gunn said.

Still hard. Always hard, when it came to the demon lurking within Angel.

Then again, so were they all. If Angel ever lost his soul to Angelus again, not even Cordelia would hesitate to stake him. Maybe especially not Cordelia.

"I'll leave stopping *whatever* up to you for now," Wesley said. He sounded distracted, the way he did when his mind had drifted away to another problem. "I've got to see if I can translate what that Tuingas fellow yelled at us. They've clearly got a beef with the faux Angel, and as long as we've been pulled into the problem, it behooves us to figure out why."

"*Behooves us,*" Gunn repeated, and snorted. "I guess it does at that. Well, translate fast, Wesley. It's morning now, but that party hearty demon night is gonna come up fast."

They drifted away from him, off to their own missions. And for a while, Angel drifted away from them, letting his preternatural healing abilities wash the rest of the Slith poison from his system. He got his toes back and more, and then there came a moment when he realized he wasn't as alone as he thought he was.

Someone turned the page of a magazine. Someone who was evidently just as able to realize he was back among the land of the functioning even though he hadn't—quite—opened his eyes yet. Cordelia said, "And then there's these two sisters who have their own show on the Discovery Health Channel. Okay, they dress kinda JCPenney, but look at them! What's not to admire? They're both respected doctors, they're pretty, they've got the sisterhood thing going, and they get to talk about sex *and* be paid for it." There was an obvious pause, after which she said, "Paid for talking about it, I mean."

"I knew that," Angel said, not quite ready to open his eyes.

"Did you?" she said, obviously not referring to the sisters.

That did it. He looked. He found her sitting in an overstuffed chair not far from the bed. It hadn't been in the bedroom before now, but she seemed quite at home in it, curled up with the magazine propped on her knees and the black chopsticks tucked behind her ear—not actually a bad strategy to keep Wesley from tap-tap-tapping them all to insanity, a state that seemed just around the bend, anyway. "Did I," he repeated flatly.

She put the magazine down against her legs, losing her place without noticing. "Go after Gunn."

He could all but see the fine line stretching out before him, that on which he had to balance. Truth . . . but not too much of it. Not enough to shatter the trust they were rebuilding. "I might have. I'm not sure."

She regarded him somberly. "That's not good."

Gingerly, he sat up, swinging his legs over the edge of the bed. Everything hurt. Everything hurt a lot. For now. "But it's okay for you to lose your temper now and then. Or Wesley, or Gunn."

"That's different. You know it is."

"That doesn't seem . . . fair."

She shrugged. "I didn't say it was."

"No." She hadn't. And it wasn't. But . . . she was right.

Angel stretched . . . rotated first one shoulder, then the other, checking the quality of light that leaked through the newspaper-taped windows. "What time is it?"

"Late morning. Wesley's frowning over his translations. Gunn's off trying to see what he can dig up about all these demons acting out—he called in a while ago; he's already been chased out of two demon dives. No answers, but they sure do seem touchy. Lorne says it's standing room only at his place. It all adds up to something . . . we just have to figure out what."

"Late morning." He grimaced. "That little spitball packed quite a punch."

She raised an eyebrow at him, very Cordelia. "If you weren't already dead, you'd be dead. Gunn's luckier than he's ever going to admit." She gave him a very wise look and said, "If you're smart, you'll leave it at that."

He was inclined to be smart.

CHAPTER TEN

The kids were all right. They put up with the rules Gunn had laid out before them: no drugs, no guns, no big talk about what they were up to. They'd even put up with his neighborhood cleanup evening—staged as much to show the neighborhood in question their good intentions as anything else—and handled their first real evidence of demon life with only one dropout.

And now they'd come up with that little detail that Angel Investigations hadn't been able to discover yet: the fake Angel's office. Gunn stared at the grimy down-under entrance, deciding to bring the others in on the first visit.

In a way, it stung. They'd done it because their life was here, because they knew the streets— and when he'd given them a description of the geek little Angel wanna-be, they'd remembered seeing him. They'd gone off with a mission . . .

and they'd come back with results.

Once upon a time, Gunn would have been the one to bring in those results. He'd known when a vampire set foot on his streets, he'd led a tight-knit gang of brothers-in-arms and he'd kept the unknowing families—the mothers and fathers and kids and grandparents and all those people tied up in what they thought was their normal little world—safe from demon violence. He hadn't even really minded when they'd looked at him and his crew with that same expression they reserved for drug dealers or gang members. It served well enough as camouflage. If no one asked questions because they were all so full of assumptions, then Gunn didn't have to answer them.

Once upon a time. Now he never knew where he'd be—in Pylea facing a whole society of green Simon Legrees, or out in the suburbs dealing with exorcisms like Hollywood had never imagined. But he could predict where he *wouldn't* be.

On his streets.

But the kids had come through. They'd done good. And that was something too.

He headed for the cell phone in his truck.

Cordelia left Angel with fresh blood and—she hoped—a lot to think about. He had to *get* it, or they'd never be able to trust him. Angel or Angelus, he had too much power . . . he had to keep it under control. He had to *get* the power of will and personality that kept them bound together as a group. It meant trusting him on a level she wasn't sure he understood.

She dropped the magazine on the counter with a sigh and sat down before the computer. Wesley might turn to his musty old books, but Cordelia had the Internet, along with the demon database they were building. She pulled up the Google search engine and typed in *demons mad attack* on the offhand chance that some lonely someone with a Web page his entire family scoffed at had actually observed something useful. Not a tactic that often worked, but sometimes . . .

You just never knew.

She skipped through a number of Web-based bulletin boards, found a cross-newsgroup flame war overwhelming any useful commentary in one of her occasionally useful haunts. She was always a lurker, picking up tidbits of truth from confused and exaggerated observations, leaving as quietly as possible. She hadn't needed Wesley's warning to keep her silence in these far-too-public venues.

"Find anything?" Angel came barefoot into the lobby, wearing his contrite face. As if she could ever resist that. He must have learned that glance-from-below thing from Princess Diana . . . or maybe he'd taught it to her.

She put up a good fight. "Lots of chatter, nothing specific. If I didn't know there was something going on, I'd be able to tell there was something going on. Not really helpful."

"How's it going with the translation?" Angel nodded at the window of Wesley's office, behind which he was bent over his desk.

"Oh, he's pretty sure the first word is the same thing the other demon said to us: 'gimme.' They want something; that's for sure."

"They want the fake *me's* client," Angel said. "That's pretty obvious."

From the office, Wesley spoke without looking up from his reading. "Yes, well, since we have no intention of handing the man over, our next best chance comes with understanding *why* they want him."

"Well, we can assume *he's* got something they want," Cordelia said, typing in the URL for the L.A. *Daily News* without paying much attention to either the keyboard or the monitor. Angel leaned over the front counter, fiddling with a giant paper clip she'd left there. "Since the word 'gimme' keeps coming up."

"Either that, or they're just selfish little bastards," Wesley muttered, just loud enough to be heard. No, the translation definitely wasn't going well. In fact, as far as she could tell, she was the only one having any kind of decent day at all.

"At least The Powers That Be have backed off on the whole vision thing," she said. "I guess we must be on the right track or some—what?" For she'd glanced at Angel, finding the paper clip twisted out of all recognizable shape in his white-knuckled hand. And his face . . . if it was possible, she'd say he'd gone pale.

She glanced at her computer monitor. Dailynews.com spread across the top of the screen in a fancy font, and below it ran breaking news headlines.

Make that *headline*. There was only one. There only needed to be one:

GANG ATTACKS GRANNY AEROBICS CLASS

On the screen was a color police sketch representative of the gang look, including a brief description. Yellow mohawk hairstyle, yellow-tinted mask. All big, all using knives. Beside it was a photo of the interior of a fitness center aerobics room, step-class equipment moved neatly to the side, yoga mats rolled up against the wall . . . pools of blood all over the floor.

"Wes," Angel said.

"Busy," Wesley said instantly.

Angel said again, *"Wes,"* and he used that rare tone of voice, one that wasn't contrite or apologetic but made it clear, in the end, who was actually in charge here at Angel Investigations.

Wesley's chair squeaked as he left his desk.

Cordelia stared at the computer monitor, horrified, her eyes filling with tears. She blinked them away, fast, so she could catch some of the details . . . morning fitness class, attacked without warning, five dead, another seven badly injured, three critically. Inexplicable gang attack, with the gang itself entirely unknown.

It had been a bloodbath.

"I saw this," she said. "A couple of nights ago, right before you took me to the clinic. I could have stopped—"

"*No*," Angel said, and he used that voice again. "You can only tell us what the visions show you. It wasn't enough."

She tried to believe him.

"Miquot," Wesley said softly, having arrived and quickly assessed the situation. "Though had anyone tried to convince me that they would stoop to such defenseless quarry, I"—he took a deep breath—"I wouldn't have believed it."

They stared for another horrified moment. Cordelia didn't even really see the monitor any longer; she didn't have to. The headline, the humanized Miquot, the bloody fitness center . . . not something she'd soon forget. As if on cue, Wes slammed a hand against the counter and jerked away, his mouth tightened on words unspoken— even as Angel stalked off, gone from contrite to predator . . . predator stalking across the lobby with no one in particular to hunt, predator close to the edge. . . .

When the phone rang, they turned back to the counter with such intensity that Cordelia hesitated as she reached for the old-fashioned handpiece. "Angel Investigations," she said in her business voice, eyeing them both. "We help the—oh, hi Gunn."

"What's wrong?" he asked immediately. The connection had a cell phone quality.

She cleared her throat. Apparently not quite as business voice as she'd intended. "Just a little tense, that's all. Whatever's got the demons around here stirred up . . . it's . . . they've . . . well, we've got to stop it, that's all there is to it."

"Dunno that I can help with that, but I think I've got that fake Angel's fake office in my sights."

"Really?" Some *good* news for a change.

"Near the corner of Fourth and Loma—a dinky little walk-down hole of a place. Thought Angel might want to be in on it."

"I think Wesley could use a little fresh air too," she said, glancing up at Wesley's grimness. He'd been struggling with the translation for too long; a little distraction—*successful* distraction—would do him good. "You'll wait for them?"

"If they get it in gear," Gunn said. "I'll wait down below, the nearest access to the corner."

"I'm sure they'll get it in gear," Cordelia said. She hung up the phone.

Instantly, Wesley said, "What? Where?"

"Fourth and Loma," Angel said, he of the keen vampire hearing.

"The faux Angel's office," Cordelia said. "Looks like you're about to do a little breaking and entering."

"Or if he's there, breaking and entering and breaking," Angel said.

She thought he was kidding.

But then again . . . maybe not.

"It looks abandoned," Wesley said, the last of them to step into the dim little office.

The dimness came partly from its small, dirty windows . . . and partly from its placement on the shady side of the street, a fact that had allowed Angel easier than normal access. Storm drains, sewers—they only went so far. He looked around the seedy room, hunting for something to help him understand just why this strange young man had gone so far in his efforts to imitate his own less than stellar self. He said, "Even that temporary office you had was better than this."

"Watch it," Gunn said. "Someone kicked us out of *his* place, remember?"

Right. He *had,* hadn't he?

"And, anyway," Gunn said, "our place had bigger windows."

"We also had bookshelves and file cabinets, as I recall," Wesley said, referring to the boxes stacked beside a rickety old metal desk. Papers spilled out, unfiled and apparently unsorted. A tilting water cooler sat by the wall, but the empty bottle had a desert-dry abandoned look to it. An open door off the back of the room revealed a tiny bathroom with a rust- and water-stained sink, and a plunger in permanent residence beneath it. The toilet ran quietly in the background. "What did that client say the first time we saw him? That this was the *main* office?"

"Yeah, well, we might as well take a look around," Angel said. The Slith poison still tingled in his veins, dulling down his receptiveness to the *angerattackrevenge* whispering through the streets . . . or maybe it was just the daylight.

"We *are* looking around," Gunn said. "Nothing and no one here. Not exactly room to hide in this place."

Angel nudged a box with his foot; it spilled onto its side, spewing papers across the floor. "Tsk," he said. "We'll have to pick that up."

"And maybe have a look at the contents while we're at it?" Wesley murmured. "Maybe we can get some idea what he's up to . . . or at least identify other clients who might be in danger under his care."

"Be nice if we could find the guy who keeps leading demons in our direction," Gunn said, a hint of promise in his voice. "Who he is, where he's staying . . ."

"And then we could have a chat with him on *our* terms," Wesley said. "Tied, for instance. So he can't run away again."

Dividing the papers up took the patience of untangling Pick Up sticks, but eventually Angel prowled the room with papers in hand, Wesley sat at the uncertain desk, and Gunn sat cross-legged on the floor, his back to the wall and his eye on the front door.

"Here's an old grade sheet," Wesley said. "David Arnnette. Some photography courses here . . . he did well in his classes."

Gunn snorted. "Doesn't make much difference if you flunk reality." He waved a small pink sheet in the air. "Here's a bill from a theatrical company—fake teeth, fake blood . . ."

"We know that much," Angel said absently. He flipped through a stack of photos. Cordelia entering the hotel, Angel himself under a streetlight, Gunn getting into his truck, him again in a bar hunting vampires . . . he held it up. "This guy's been watching me for a while."

"How did he even find out about you?" Wesley said. "That's what I want to know."

"Here," Angel said, flipping to the bottom of the photos. "Look at this one. Nighttime, alley . . . the oldest one here. I dusted some vamps. Didn't even know he was there."

"There are always witnesses," Wesley said.

"And they're usually so frightened or drunk or hurt that they don't have any trouble convincing themselves they didn't see what they thought they saw," Angel said. "Hundreds of years haven't changed that. Or streetlights."

"Except this one had a camera."

"Yes," Wesley said slowly, taking the oldest picture from Angel. "This one had a camera." He looked up. "This was when Doyle was still alive?"

"Before Cordelia even got here," Angel said. "Whatever obsession this guy has, he's been nursing it a while."

"Then I suppose we're lucky it hasn't caused trouble before now."

"Huh," Gunn said, fumbling with an open manila file folder as eight-by-ten glossies slipped out. He caught them, shuffled them back into order, and held one up for them. "Here's a strange one. What *is* this?"

Taken from above, it showed a leg surrounded by a metal brace system that looked like nothing less than a torture device.

"I've seen those," Wesley said. "It's a bone-stabilizing brace. It's used to lengthen limbs."

"Make the whole leg longer, you mean," Gunn said, and made a face at the device. "No, thank you."

Angel said, "Looks like the photographer was the one wearing it."

Wesley nodded and gave the photo another

thoughtful look. "Then our faux Angel wasn't always light on his feet."

"You think he had a short leg?" Gunn said. "And then what, got himself fixed and decided to become a superhero, make up for all those years of being picked last in gym?"

"Too bad he's not any good at it," Angel said. Abruptly, he stopped his prowling, focusing his attention on the half-glass, half-wood door. "Did you hear—"

The door burst open, entirely without the benefit of anyone turning the doorknob; glass flexed and broke, spraying the office. Wesley jumped away from the desk as Gunn sprang to his feet, each groping for the weapons they'd set aside.

In the doorway stood a man, or what was mostly a man. Draped over his head and shoulders like a flexible living cloak—a nearly invisible one at that—something pulsed and breathed; below it, the man's eyes held a maniacal look, unrestrained fervor and intent. "Where's Angel?" he bellowed. "I'm going to kill him!"

Angel looked at the man and his unusual fashion accessory, looked at the door, and made a disapproving noise at both. "It's a bad week for doors."

"It's quiet," Fred said. She ran a finger along the brass inlays of the stair railing, frowning slightly. "I like it when it's quiet."

"You don't look like you like it," Cordelia observed. She was scouring the L.A. news sites, marking down the unusual incidents, plotting them on a map. So far, the majority of them had been in Westlake.

"Well, the other thing is that when it's quiet, my head feels noisy," Fred admitted. "Thoughts forget to take their turn. Unlike, say, if Angel is here, and he's talking, then thoughts about what he's saying get to come first, before all those thoughts on how to open a portal and get back home."

Cordelia looked up, discovering it was her turn to frown. She quickly schooled away the bumpy brow effect. "But . . . you *are* home."

"Oh, I know that," Fred responded, casually self-assured in a strangely normal moment. "But you know, when you've been thinking about one thing so hard for so long, it doesn't just go away."

"Maybe you should write it down," Cordelia offered. "All your . . . well, calculations and stuff. Maybe that would help."

"Oh, I write them down," Fred said. "Or not *down* exactly . . ."

Cordelia gave her a sharp glance, once again getting the feeling that Fred meant something slightly different from the obvious—but Fred had gone vague again, and Cordelia left her to it. The question was, were all these incidents along Alvarado coincidental—the flock of Slith in

MacArthur Park among them—or did the pattern mean something?

"Cordelia," Fred said, and her voice was not vague in the least. More like wary.

Cordelia couldn't help her exasperation, anyway. "Fred, I'm trying to—oh, hello."

For there in the lobby stood their faux Angel. He'd obviously come in down below, through what Cordelia thought as *their* Angel's private entrance. He gave a little wave.

She put her hands on her cocked hips and said, "I sure hope you don't have any bad guys dogging your tail, because I'm fresh out of save-the-day coupons."

"Not as far as I know. Anyway, they're after Lutkin, not me."

"Yeah, that makes a whole lot of difference to us when they're breaking down our doors to get here. Which you *will* pay for, by the way. This hotel is a historical landmark, not your own personal trouble palace!"

"As if you people needed any help in *that* department," he snorted.

"Just what do you know about it?" she shot back at him.

He took a step back, and seemed suddenly startled . . . more by himself, she would have said, than by any comment of her own. "Enough," he said. "I know enough."

"Enough to set yourself up as Angel Investigations, undercutting our business and luring God knows how many unsuspecting people into placing their confidence in you? This is serious work, you know. We're not just playing games here." She swept her gaze up and down his body. Still in basic black, although he'd loosened his belt enough so his jeans were no longer cinched up around his waist. "You know, even Angel varies the look. Last week I caught him in a cranberry sweater."

"Dark cranberry," Fred offered.

"Even so." She waved a hand at him, indicating the clothes, the hair. "The black, the duster, way too much hair gel . . . and have you got *eyeliner* on? Going for the dramatic look?"

"No, of course not," he said. He didn't sound convincing, and she wasn't convinced.

"So what's this all about, anyway?" She nodded at him. "The look. The business. Don't you have your own life? You have to use someone else's?"

Fred stood up, wrapping her hands around the railing as she looked down at him. "That's it, isn't it? You just wanted to leave your old life behind."

Caught between them, he hesitated, mouth open.

"I've done that, by the way," Fred added. "It doesn't really work out like you think it will."

"You're wrong there," he said, finding his voice again. With emphasis. "It's working out just fine. People know

I'm *someone* now—not something to be ignored. They look *at* me, not through me. Or away from me, like they're too embarrassed to even see me. I've got power, now. People are afraid of me."

"I'm not." Fred had that earnest, honest little voice, one that said she was trying to be helpful even when she said exactly the wrong thing. It took the faux Angel aback a moment.

"I'm not either," Cordelia said, with no intent to be helpful at all. "And you're all wrong, imitating Angel so you can feel *powerful*. So people will be afraid of you. That's not what he's about at all."

"You don't think so?" Faux Angel snorted. "I've got plenty of evidence to the contrary."

"Angel *helps* people," Fred said. "Boy, you really *are* messed up. Try writing things down. It helps."

Frustrated, he crossed his arms across his chest in a most defiant posture and scowled at them. "You don't know anything about me, and you must not know much about other people, if you think this whole demon-hunting gig is about *helping* people. It's about what it makes *you*. And that's *not* what I came here to talk about!"

They exchanged scowls for a moment, and then Cordelia realized, "You knew he wouldn't be here. You knew it would just be me." She glanced at the stairs and added hastily, "Me and Fred. So what is it you want? Because you're wasting my time, and I'm busy."

"It's only fair, really," Fred said. "Considering the guys are at his place right now."

"Fred!"

"So they found it," Faux Angel said, a little grimly. "It was bound to happen. It doesn't matter. You can't stop me from being who I am."

"And we're not trying to," Cordelia said, with the sudden impression she was being way too reasonable with a madman. "We want you to stop being who *Angel* is."

"We're indistinguishable at this point."

"Oh," Cordelia said, as pointedly as possible. "I wouldn't go that far." She straightened abruptly, waving him off with a shooing motion. "Well, this has been fun, but like I said, I'm busy. Go away now. Go rinse that dye out of your hair, and contemplate the bright cheerful colors brought to us by fall fashions."

He shrugged, and turned to go . . . but hesitated, looking over his shoulder with a calculating glance that made Cordelia wary.

And rightly so.

He said, "Then I guess you don't want to know what has the demons in this city all stirred up."

From the back entry came another voice. Smooth. Dark and low. Full of the power and influence Faux Angel coveted so badly.

"Actually," Angel said, "I guess we do."

• • •

The imposter almost bolted. Again. But as he hesitated, even as Angel prepared himself for a chase, Cordelia put herself before the remains of the front door, and Gunn, having parked his truck, came in through the courtyard entrance. Angel detected Fred sitting quietly on the stairs, being not-noticed.

From behind Angel, Wesley said, "No—wait—"

The demon-draped man pushed up behind Angel, who put a casual hand against the wall just in time to block him. "That's him!" the man said. "You didn't tell me you had him here! I'm going to—"

"Wait quietly," Angel said, his voice full of meaning. "Because if Wes is too busy saving that man's butt, he won't be able to help *you*, will he?"

"But that fake deserves to—"

"I have no doubt," Wes muttered. "Come along. You can wait in my office. Would you like a soda?"

"Cherry cola would be nice," the man admitted. "Or a root beer."

Watching the demon-draped man settle meekly into Wesley's office, Faux Angel finally found his voice. "What's this all about?" he asked. "I've never seen that man before."

"Sure you have," Angel said, keeping all intensity out of his voice. He felt better now, the Slith poison washed out of his quick-healing system, the anger creeping back in. But now was not the time for anger.

Maybe in a few moments.

"The thing is, Dave—can I call you Dave, by the way?—the thing is, 'that man' came to you as a customer of what he thought was Angel Investigations. But he looks a little different from when you saw him."

"How's that?" the faux Angel—David Arrnette— asked warily.

"The thing *is*," Wesley said, rummaging in the refrigerator and straightening with two soda cans in his hands, "the man had a demon problem. Something living in the tree in his backyard? Teasing his dog, leaving droppings everywhere, ripping clothes off the line . . . is this sounding familiar yet?"

A puzzled look settled on Faux Angel's thin features. "But I took care of that."

Angel prowled closer to his imitator. "Well, no," he said, sounding what he thought was fairly reasonable. He wasn't sure why the man flinched. "In fact, you didn't. What you did was to rush out to his yard—"

"Having done no research whatsoever," Wesley inserted, putting the soda cans on the counter. Neither one was cherry cola or root beer.

"And use perfectly ordinary means—what was it, a twenty-two rifle? Had to have been something small, or the neighbors would have reacted—to take care of the thing in the tree."

In the office, the man quit playing with the

chopsticks and yelled, "I was better off with the thing in the tree! You charlatan!"

Wesley quickly gathered the soda. "I think I'd better just—"

"You might want to close the door," Cordelia advised him, still standing guard by the front entrance, arms crossed and hip cocked and not looking at all like someone who was only just starting self-defense work in the basement. "Because really, I think we're still getting over the last cleaning job, don't you?"

"I killed the thing," Faux Angel said defiantly to Angel. "What's the big deal?"

Gunn, standing solidly by the courtyard door and looking very much like someone who's done self-defense work in the basement all his life, said, "The big deal is that it wasn't *one* creature, it was *two*. And unless you kill it with electricity, you're better off spraying the tree with dogz-be-gone."

"That would work?" Faux Angel asked suspiciously. "Dogz-be-gone?"

"The creature has a highly developed sense of smell," Angel said. "But since you didn't do your research and you didn't use electricity to kill it and you didn't just drive it away, you left its companion alive. And its companion found a new friend."

"Wonder what that was like," Gunn said. He moved toward the center of the lobby, where their visitor shifted uncomfortably. "Can you imagine, sleeping all nice and cozy in your own bed, thinking your yard is clear and your house is safe, and then from out of *nowhere*—" He nodded at Wesley's office.

Beyond the big glass window, the man sat uncomfortably, the jellyfish of a demon hugging his shoulders, oozing slightly around his neck. Every now and then he shrugged, an unconscious effort to dislodge the creature; it only clung tighter.

The faux Angel made a face, wrinkling his nose in disgust—then caught himself and schooled his features to the remote interest of someone who couldn't possibly be to blame. "What's it doing?"

"Absorbing nutrients of some sort, I would think," Fred said from the stairs, breaking her long silence. "But what the normal host demon provided as nutrient may be something it's not a good thing for that man to lose."

"Can you get it off before it—" Faux Angel couldn't quite bring himself to say it.

"Before it kills him?" Gunn said, and Faux Angel winced.

"Wes is good," Cordelia said simply.

"And you," Angel said, moving close, "are not. You're not me. You're not *us*. You wanna play with demons? Fine. But do it under your own name, *Dave*."

Faux Angel looked at the floor. "David," he said. "I prefer David."

Cordelia eased in from the entrance, apparently deciding the flight risk moment was over. "So," she said casually, "you were going to tell us what has everything all stirred up."

The reminder wasn't a welcome one to Angel; fresh awareness made for a fresh assault on emotions grown raw. Nor did it help his mood when Faux Ang—*David*—put on his well-practiced sullen look. David said, "You're the ones who're so good at research. Maybe you should just figure it out."

Angel said instantly, "Or maybe I should just—"

Gunn narrowed his eyes. It was enough. Angel subsided.

Cordelia ignored them both. She said to David, "Just stop with the attitude. Trust me, we've seen enough of the real thing that you're just boring us. And you know, we might actually *have* things figured out by now—if we didn't keep getting interrupted by Tuingas demons."

"Tuingas?" David repeated as Wesley reemerged from the office; this time he was careful to close the door behind him. "I mean, of course, the Tuingas."

Pushing past Angel and Gunn, Cordelia moved right up on David, poking him in the chest, driving him backward until one of the roundchairs caught him behind the knees and he abruptly sat into it. "Yes, the Tuingas. And let me tell you something, bud . . . between the Tuingas and the mysterious

183

whatever that has every demon within shouting distance of downtown looking for trouble, I've been nonstop Vision Girl. And I'm taking that *really personally*, if you get my drift. So whatever you know about either of them, fess up!"

At this, David did look truly confused. "But they're pretty much the same thing. Didn't you know that?"

"What part of *not know* did you not understand?" she asked him.

"It makes sense," Wesley said slowly. "We saw the first demon—and your client—about the same time these unusual incidents started. Humble demons turning aggressive, demons who make a big deal out of hunting big game go for a bunch of grandmothers

David seemed to shrink back in the chair. "That . . . they said that was a gang—"

"No," Wesley said shortly, and then hesitated, softening somewhat. "I'm sorry to tell you it was several Miquot. Feel free to read up on them . . . the Cliff's Notes version would tell you simply that they're the Terminators of the demon world. Those elderly women didn't stand a chance."

"But—"

"I'm sorry." Wesley looked like he might actually feel bad for the imposter. "There's really no doubt."

Angel didn't feel bad for him at all. "So it's time for you to quit stalling and—"

"It's my client," David said abruptly. "Lutkin. It's got something to do with him. I suspected it might—he's in the Alvarado Palms Hotel, and—"

"That's just down the street from MacArthur Park," Gunn said.

"And near the post office," Wes said.

"Above the spot where that Oua'shin attacked the boy," Angel added.

"Right," David said. "I mean, some of the stuff has been spread out, but most of it—at least what I know of—has been pretty close to the Alvarado. The end that Lutkin is staying on."

"That fits what I've put together . . . so tell us about Lutkin." Cordelia plopped down on the roundchair next to David, but it was hardly a companionable move. More like not-so-subtle impatience. Angel couldn't blame her—she'd already had her quota of vision-headaches, and they weren't near to solving this thing yet.

The faux Angel shifted uneasily away from her and pushed his glasses up his nose. "I don't know all that much," he warned. "He came to me looking for protection. He said he'd gained the attention of some demons and that it should only last a few days, maybe a week. He's done something to his room, so he's safe there . . . he just calls me when he wants to go out. Or, well"—he shrugged—"when he wants an escort. I get the impression he's been out and about on his own, and there have been a few times he's ditched me."

"Like when he showed up here with a Tuingas demon on his tail," Gunn said.

"That was one of them," David admitted. "It's taken me a few days, but I finally figured out—I mean, I think he's got something they want."

Gunn somehow seemed to look a little bigger in his impatience. "Uh-huh. Still waiting for more stuff we don't know."

"*That's* never good news," Cordelia said, talking over Gunn. "It's always some object of power, and you just *know* if they get their hands on it, there'll be an apocalypse or something."

"Or something," Wesley agreed, rather grimly. "And he's given you no indication of what this object might be?"

"Hey," David said, "he hasn't even admitted that he's got anything. But either he's got something, or it's *him,* because all this started when he got here, and it's all centered around him. The things that haven't gone down near the Alvarado . . . well, except for the granny thing, I can place him in the area. And for all I know, he was there."

Angel felt an uncomfortable prickle of conscience. *Tell them,* it said. *Tell them what you've been feeling. Tell them how it's spread. How it's gotten stronger.* Even so, he hesitated—except Cordelia was already looking at him, her eyes narrowed ever so slightly. She said flatly, "What?"

Angel cleared his throat. "I was just going to say . . . not necessarily. That this fellow is where the trouble is, I mean. Maybe to start with . . . but not necessarily anymore."

"What do you mean?" Wesley asked, catching on to the fact that Faux Angel wasn't the only one making confessions in the lobby and not looking entirely happy about it.

"It's just that . . . there's been something—an influence, a psychic emanation—in the air. You know that," he said, glancing at Gunn and Wesley. He'd told them . . . he just hadn't told them everything. "It's been driving demons into Caritas. But . . . it's been growing stronger. And it's worse at night. It may have started out as tied to Lutkin's location, but I think it's gone beyond that now."

"You *knew* about Lutkin and this thing?" Gunn asked, drawing himself up.

Almost simultaneously, Wesley said, "What do you mean, 'growing stronger'?"

"No!" Angel said. "I mean, I knew there was something affecting demons. I didn't have any idea it was connected to this Lutkin fellow. And yeah, it's growing stronger."

"Do we want to know how you know this?"

ANGEL

Gunn asked. "Or was that little comment in Caritas supposed to be enough of a clue?"

"How do you think he knows it?" Cordelia said. "Why do you think he nearly went for you, Gunn?"

"*Did* go for me," Gunn growled.

"Not in the end," she said, sounding unperturbed . . . unless you looked in her eyes. The very eyes that now drilled suspicion at Angel. "But he could have. How about it, Angel? Are you the next *demon incident* on the list?"

Angel badly wanted a drink. A nice, warm, copper-tanged drink. But he thought this was probably the exact wrong time. He let them all look at him a while, and let them see that he wasn't going to explode or turn evil or buckle under their scrutiny. He said, "I've been dealing with this kind of conflict for a long, long time. I can handle it. I *am* handling it. These others . . . these demons aren't used to fighting an outside influence. Or an inside influence. They . . . just don't know how. They may not even realize it's happening."

"But you did," Cordelia said. She was never the one to let him off the hook. "You did, and you didn't say anything to us."

He hesitated but, in the end, nodded. "I *did*," he said. "And I didn't. I . . . was afraid of how you'd take it."

"We *have* rather made a big thing about dependability lately," Wesley said. And Angel relaxed a fraction, thinking maybe this wouldn't be so bad, until Wesley added, "You know, dependability. Such as telling the truth, being forthright with your comrades, not hiding things that could affect those comrades—"

"Hey!" Angel said, stung. "You ever consider the no-win-ness of this situation? You want me all nice and tame and predictable, and I've tried to be those things in spite of whatever's going on here. Now you're mad because I didn't tell you I wasn't feeling predictable. What would you have been if I *had?* Giving me the eye, watching me, second-guessing me—"

"We're going to do that now, anyway," Gunn said.

"Then I made the right choice, didn't I?" Angel told him. "I saved myself actual *days* of it."

"He's right, you know," Cordelia said, so suddenly it sent Faux Angel scooting a couple more inches away in alarm. "I mean, I'm the last person to say so and I'll be the first person to walk away if I think you're going to pull more of that *I'm going to save you by being awful to you* crap, but . . . in this situation? Nothing you would have done would have been right." She gave him a thoughtful look, nodding quietly to herself. "Yep. You're just going to have to get used to being wrong."

They all looked at one another for a long moment while Angel thought of his years as a vampire and all he'd done and how it never let go of him. He said, "Used to that, too."

No one did much to acknowledge that, but no one argued it either. Gunn said, "What's it add up to, then? Lutkin has something the Tuingas want. And it has something to do with the bad vibes that're whipping these demons up into a frenzy."

"That's all you know?" Wesley asked the faux Angel.

David shrugged. "I know he's going out again tonight—late. He wants me along. I get the feeling he pretty much expects trouble . . . he told me to get extra help."

"So you came *here*?" Gunn asked, rather incredulously.

David shrugged, unabashed.

"Who knows, maybe he'll come here himself," Cordelia said. "He's been here twice already. And he doesn't seem to mind playing us off each other."

"He's been playing us from the start, and I've had enough," the faux Angel said, scowling. But after a moment's thought, he gave a decisive shake of his head. "I don't think he'll be back. He's still counting on me, but I think he's figured out that you might not exactly consider him the good guy."

"With good reason," Wesley said. "But it certainly makes it difficult to pick his brains."

Cordelia winced. "I'm not sure that's a phrase you should use around here."

"Feeling a little literal?" Wesley asked. And then, "Never mind. Let's give Lorne a call. If our false Angel here can't tell us any more, perhaps the details we have will jog something in Lorne's memory. Other than that, it's back to the books."

Cordelia left the roundchair and slipped back behind the front counter to pick up the phone. "Auto-dialing is such a wonderful thing, don't you think? Too bad we don't have it. Hi," she said into the phone. "Need to talk to Lorne. He's in a what?" she said. And, "Oh. Well, if he wakes up, ask him to call."

"How's that?" Wesley asked as she hung up.

"He's in a coma," she said, picking up a pen and fiddling with it. "Or something. Too much emotional input, although I guess they disconnected the karaoke machine. Hard to tell. Whatever's tending bar . . . doesn't really sound like it has a mouth."

"Then all we know is that Lutkin has something he probably shouldn't, he's going somewhere tonight, and he expects trouble," Angel said, startling them all somewhat. Too rational, perhaps. "We can stake out the hotel."

David said uncertainly, "If he spots you . . . ," and then shook his head. More assertively, he said, "Let me call you, when I find out where we're going. I know it's going to be late in the evening."

"Uh-huh," Gunn said. "So we're supposed to trust you now, is that it?"

David looked at each of them, and found Gunn's sentiment echoed in Wesley's raised eyebrow, and in Cordelia's crossed arms and tightened lips. Angel merely stared back at him, reflecting nothing. The faux Angel stood up and patted his pockets and eventually pulled out a business card—one that looked just like their own, with a different phone number. "Here," he said. "That's my cell. Call me. That's even better—I won't have to sneak away, I'll just take a call from another client like normal. Call me every half hour, call me every fifteen minutes, I don't care."

"Every fifteen minutes might be a little excessive," Wesley said dryly, taking the card. "But you can count on hearing from us."

"Good," David said. "Look, I . . . I'm in over my head here. I'm not gonna let you down on this, because I think you're my only hope of getting through it without more trouble than there's already been."

"Keep it in mind," Gunn said.

The faux Angel nodded, and looked at the back of the hotel with the obvious intent to make his exit.

"Use the front doors, will you?" Angel asked. "Or what's left of them. You won't burst into flame . . . be thankful for it."

David hesitated, then did as asked. When he was well and truly gone, Angel said flatly, "Watch Lutkin?"

Gunn was already in motion. "I'm on it," he said. "I'll let you know when they make their move."

"Remember," Angel said. "Things with the demons . . . get worse at night."

CHAPTER ELEVEN

Gunn was more than *on it*. He put the kids on it. He parked his truck north of the Alvarado Palms— just too far north to see the hotel itself, close enough to make it only a few moments' walk away—and called Sinthea on his cell. "I've got a job for you. A hotel I need watched."

Without missing a beat, she said, "This sounds more like *Gunn plays his homies into free scut work* than a neighborhood"—and here she did hesitate, clearly not entirely certain she wouldn't be overheard as she lowered her voice and finished—"demon watch."

"You want in on what drove those Slith to attack us the other night?" he asked.

Another hesitation, this time with a different feel to it. "Yeah?" she said eventually. "This have anything to do with those old folks who were killed? That didn't feel right. And Rosalba's *abuela* was at that gym."

"Same deal," he told her. "We're tracking the guy who's behind it." Or at least the guy who seemed to be behind it. He wasn't sure how much stock he wanted to put in either the word or the conclusions of the strange man so eager to claim Angel's name. "We've got word he's leaving the Alvarado Palms this evening and he'll have . . . well, this thing we need to get back from him."

"Not telling, huh," she said, sounding distant again.

Gunn waited for an approaching ambulance to speed past in a Doppler effect of changing siren noise, and said, "It's not a trust thing. It's a *we're still figuring it out* thing. It comes down to this: We need to know when he leaves that hotel, and he knows what all of our people look like. I'll be here the whole time, just not where he can see me."

"Or you can see him," she said.

"That's how it goes, yeah."

"How's that friend of yours?" she said. "The one who saved you?"

Not a casual inquiry. He said, "He'll be all right." *Unless this damned stone thing, whatever it's doing, gets to him along with the rest of the demons around here.* Definitely a possibility.

"I guess we owe him," she said.

I guess if things had been just a little different, you might be on his tail. But out loud, Gunn said, "Are you in, then? Are your people in?"

That got to her, as he'd meant it to. Giving respect to her own authority among the kids. She said, "You want us to watch the hotel."

"Split it up into short shifts," he said, staring down a street tough who seemed to think Gunn shouldn't be parked in that spot, talking on his phone. They exchanged nothing more than glare through window glass, but this one was a poser and moved on. Gunn didn't let it put so much as a hitch in his conversation. "Shouldn't be past midnight," he said. "*Evening* is the word I hear, so you've got some time to pull them together. And like I said, I'll be right here."

"All right," she said. "Gotta make some calls."

"Good." Gunn was about to pull the phone from his ear when it occurred to him to say, "Hey—you see any big ugly things with no necks and what looks like elephant trunks sticking out of its throats, you guys stay far away from them. They want what we want, and they want it worse."

She paused; he could hear her soft laugh. "Kinda gives new meaning to the phrase 'ear, nose, and throat man,' doesn't it?"

He smiled in spite of himself, but it didn't last long. "I'm not kidding. These guys don't seem to go out of their way to hurt people, so if you keep your distance, you should be all right. You get full of yourself and try to prove anything, and your people will end up someone else's people—you get me?"

"Sure," she said lightly. "See you there, Gunn."

Too lightly, he thought. Unlike the faux Angel, these kids didn't want to take their cues from anyone.

Not even the one who'd gotten them into this . . . and knew how to keep them safe.

Cordelia gave Angel some time alone and then went hunting him. An unpleasant alarm gave her that just-ate-way-too-much Ben & Jerry's feeling in the pit of her stomach when she found his suite empty, but a glance at the angle of light on the papered-over windows of the suite revealed that late afternoon had arrived, and that meant he had a heavily shaded nook in the courtyard if he chose to take it. If he'd wanted, he could have walked right behind her to get there and she wouldn't have known it . . . and probably had.

So she went back downstairs and through the lobby with its weird color scheme of old green walls and dark red flooring with a wavy pattern that must have been a leftover art nouveau impulse on the part of the original owners. Through the huge window of Wes's office, she spotted the demon-draped man napping with his head on the desk while Wes approached it with a book in hand and a look of great determination on his face. Not something she thought she needed to be in on. Or, more to the point, *wanted* to be in on.

She found Angel sitting on a white painted iron patio chair in the deep shade of the small boxy courtyard, staring at the fountain—not turned on today, which made it a pretty boring view—and in full brood mode.

"Look," she said, massaging an aching temple, "if anyone's brooding, it should be me. I'm the one who's had visions set to *full speed ahead* for days now. And if David What'shisface is right, it's only going to get worse—at least until we do something about his client. To think, we had him right under our noses—twice!—and didn't do anything about it."

"We didn't know," Angel said, but his words were rote.

"You're out here thinking about that David guy," Cordelia said in wise assessment. "You're thinking how messed up he is to be admiring and imitating the vampire who was once the scourge of Europe. Well, let me just get it out of the way for you: You're right. He's messed up."

"*Hey,*" he said, stung into looking at her.

"Oh, don't get me wrong," she said. "It's not because he picked you to imitate. You've got to keep in mind the way people are, Angel. You know . . .

mortal and all that. Short-lived. Focused on the moment. At the moment, you're *not* the horrible, soulless creature who tortured women and killed children and—"

"*Got the picture,*" he said, turning a glance of warning on her.

"Okay, right, you were there," she said quickly, squelching a slightly nervous laugh. "Anyway, the point is . . . here and now? You're on the other side. You're right in the thick of it. You know, do-gooding, rescuing people, being all heroic and everything. The thing is, this David guy isn't paying attention to that stuff. He doesn't know about your past, and he doesn't care about what you're *really* about. . . . He's on a power trip."

"He's what?" Angel said, startled enough to be truly responsive.

"Power trip," she said. "He doesn't care about helping people. He cares about some fake power rush that comes along with the reputation of someone who battles demons and happens to help people along the way. He cares about the money, and he cares about the influence he thinks it gives him."

After a moment, Angel said, "We care about the money."

"True," she said bluntly, which was really one of her best traits. Plain-speaking. "But not for the sake of having it." *At least, not anymore, although this poor-little-once-rich girl still has some serious shopping envy attacks.* "Just because in order to do what we really want—stop bad guys, follow visions to help the helpless, yada yada yada—we've got to have a certain amount of it to work with."

"Are you homing in on any sort of point here?"

"Be nice. I've got a compact, and I can reflect all sorts of sunlight right onto your flammable body," she told him, glad to see he was paying enough attention to wince. "The point is, this guy's got his head screwed on crooked and he's imitating you for all the wrong reasons. You're wasting your time sitting out here brooding over how you're not good enough to be a role model. David's not really interested in the good parts, anyway."

"Oh," Angel said, looking surprised and thoughtful.

And then, just as Cordelia was mentally patting herself on the back with both hands, he added, "That's not what I was doing, though."

"You weren't?"

He shook his head. "No," he said, and looked back out onto the sunlight that splashed against the courtyard's far walls. The shadows had crept up ever since Cordelia's arrival. "The . . . emanations. Whatever they are—"

"The thing that's driving all the demons around here mad, you mean," she said.

"Unless there are other emanations around here that I don't know about yet, yes. Those." He looked up to meet her gaze solidly; it rocked her slightly, as it often did. "They're getting worse. Much worse. I just thought that if I came out here, if I looked at the sunlight . . . if I got close to it—"

"You thought it would help," she said flatly, hiding the instant resurgence of that feeling in the pit of her stomach.

"I hoped," he said, but his voice was bleak enough to let her know how badly he'd needed that help, and how short the courtyard sunlight had fallen in providing it.

"Oh," she said, unable to hide her dread this time.

After a moment, in an entirely different tone, he said, "But just so we're straight—that guy doesn't really look like me in that outfit of his, does he? I mean, the hair's gotta be all wrong. And my pants—"

"Oh," she said, all quick reassurance and relief at once. This was the Angel she knew, so entirely clueless about his effect on people and his appearance. "No, no, your ankles hardly ever show at all, and when they do you've usually got that sockless Sonny Crockett thing going, so it's fine. Really."

He settled back into the chair, muttering, "Good."

She left him like that, feeling lighter and even happy to know that he seemed to have moved on from the whole *I am not worthy* obsession, at least as his major downer focus of the day. She even felt cheerful at the prospect of tackling Wesley's odd new resource book again, seeing as he was plenty busy with the demon-draped man.

All the same, she'd heard what Angel had said. Tonight would be a bad one for the demons of L.A., for the people who fought them . . . and for Angel.

Khundarr felt the strength of the stone build . . . he felt the beginning wobble of its instability. As it sent out waves of emotion to the demon population, so it received them in kind . . . new impressions, increasing its powerful effect on those in the city as it drove them toward disaster. Los Angeles had withstood riots and earthquakes and raging rainy season floods and mud slides, and proudly thought it could withstand just about anything.

Those in the city had no idea.

As darkness fell, Khundarr left his underpass hideout and headed north on Alvarado to the hotel where the stone's false keeper kept it hidden. The protections laid on the place might not let Khundarr enter, but sooner or later the man would again leave the dwelling, giving Khundarr another chance at him.

If only the humans from the other hotel had the

wisdom to understand they were protecting the wrong thing. They were protecting the thief, and not their own city. Or perhaps not a thief exactly—given that the young Tuingas had created the unfortunate circumstances under which the deathstone had entered this world—but certainly a man who knew what he had . . . and knew he shouldn't have it. If only that motley group of humans hadn't been so good at protecting those whom they chose, rightly or wrongly, to protect. . . . Khundarr never would have predicted the death of the youngster—never mind Kaalesh—killed by the vampire.

They were not entirely without wit; twice they had chosen not to pursue him when he'd made it obvious he was in retreat. He considered himself lucky that the vampire had only wounded him, given that the once-man was as bombarded by the deathstone emanations as the rest of the city's demon populace. And he had the feeling the humans understood he was making efforts to communicate. . . .

But their response could not help but be too little, too late. They didn't have the resources to fully understand their own predicament, or Khundarr's obligations. If they managed, somehow, to be of help to him, he could be nothing but grateful. But if they got in the way again . . . innocents or no, he could not hold back.

• • •

Gunn lurked in an alley away from the hotel and down by the corner of Twelfth Place, loitering with practiced ease . . . although he wished he could at least *watch* the kids as they watched the hotel. His cell phone rang every forty minutes or so as darkness fell around him, and the kids coming off watch made a point of stopping by to let him see how casually effective they were being.

Tyree and Sinthea had assigned short shifts to everyone who wanted one—and once they learned they were helping to solve the granny murders, everyone did—but they themselves hung around conspicuously in the background, holding on to their authority and drifting by Gunn every now and then so he'd be sure to know it.

He thought they were far too new to this gig to be so assured. . . . They didn't yet know what they didn't know.

They came around the corner again, sharing some comment that gave them both pleased, cocky expressions. Sinthea was hardly dressed in a way to remain inconspicuous, with her slender waist exposed by a knit crop-top, and her jeans hanging way down on her hips, ultra-low. Tyree's jeans were almost as low, on lean hips that held them up through friction or magic or double-sided tape. Gunn had once experimented with the big and baggy and low look. That same week he'd caught an episode of *Cops* on television and had seen how quickly those pants slipped right off when it came to a real scuffle. Floundering around with his pants at his ankles didn't seem to be the best strategy to staying alive as he kept the streets safe, so he'd given them away the next day.

"Next time we get up a meeting, we'll talk about how *not* to attract attention," he muttered, slouching deceptively by the side of a weed-edged brick building. "And how keeping your *look* isn't nearly as important as keeping your life."

Tyree gave him a *look*, all right.

Sinthea seemed amused by both the comment and Tyree's reaction. She flipped her hair back over her shoulder and said, "We're here doing your work for you, aren't we? What's to complain?"

"Complain?" Gunn said, and frowned at her. "When I've got a complaint, you'll know it. What I've *got* is experience."

"Whatever," she said. "You want the news, or what?"

Now *that* was a whole different story. Gunn straightened; it was enough for Sinthea. She said, "He just left. He met a geeky guy trying to look proud in black, and they were headed for a taxi—" Her eyes widened, almond-shaped surprise in her sleekly angled face. An instant without posturing, and an expression that quickly spread to Tyree's harsher features.

Gunn turned and found himself several yards away from a Tuingas demon. "Whoa," he said. "That's not good."

Tyree recovered enough to put his tough face back on. "Get it!" he said. "Or get outta my way so I can—"

But Gunn wasn't so sure that *getting it* was the best option. He'd seen these things in battle . . . he knew what it took to defeat one. He hadn't exactly brought an arsenal along, not for a simple stakeout. Or rather, he had an arsenal—he *always* had an arsenal—but it was back in the truck. "Just hold on," he said, putting a hand out behind him, spreading it open in front of Tyree's chest but careful to leave him room. The wrong prod, and Tyree would feel obliged to charge into the fight regardless.

"Just hold on," he repeated as the Tuingas stood quietly, almost . . . thoughtfully. Its second, trunk-like nose waved gently before it, questing for scents, and though Gunn saw weapons in its wide sash, the demon made no move for them. "I dunno that this guy's on our side . . . but I'm not sure he's against us either."

"What do you mean?" Sinthea sounded scared. Good.

"Are you nuts?" Tyree asked, putting scorn into the question. "How much more *demon* can you get than that?"

"Not a whole lot," Gunn admitted.

"This is the kind you told me to watch out for," Sinthea said. "That you told me to stay *away* from."

"This is it," he said. "My guess is, it's here for the same reason we are. It wants what we want . . . whatever it is that Lutkin has. The question is, which is worse for us—if Lutkin has it, or if these demons have it?" Man, it would be so much easier if Wesley would just figure out what it was the demons kept shouting at them. . . .

Or not shouting. For this demon, as it understood Gunn's intent to stay his hand, quietly and distinctly repeated the words it had shouted in the hotel. Definitely the same one, even in this uneven streetlight . . . that distinctive wound pretty much said it all. "Okay," Gunn said to it. "I get that. And we're trying to figure out what you want. But you'd better know . . . we're going to stop you if we think you need stopping."

"Stop him *now*," Tyree said tensely.

Gunn gave a sharp shake of his head. "Not if he's the best chance we have of turning off the demon temper tantrums that have been going on." And with Lutkin as the epicenter of the tantrums and the Tuingas fixated on Lutkin. . . .

"But you don't know that he *is*," the youth argued. "He might just be making it all worse!"

"Yup," Gun agreed as the Tuingas backed a step, taking a careful look at Sinthea and Tyree until

Sinthea, tough as she was, eased a step closer to Gunn. "If it turns out that way, then we kill him." He glanced back at Tyree, a meaningful look. "But not until we *know*."

"Well, you'd better figure it out," Sinthea said, sounding shaken at this first face-to-face with blatant demonliness but regaining her determination fast. "Because by now, that guy you wanted watched has found himself a taxi."

Gunn muttered a curse, and dug carefully into his generous front pocket, not taking his eyes off the Tuingas. He found his ridiculously small cell phone and flipped it open, glancing down just long enough to hit the auto-dial sequence for the Hyperion.

When he looked up again, the demon was gone; the kids behind him had stiffened at the ease with which it had faded into the darkness. Gunn didn't waste time worrying about it, not with Cordelia's tense greeting in his ear. "It's me," he said. "Lutkin and Arnnette are on the—"

"—Move!" Cordelia cried, dropping the front desk phone as the vision hit. "Move, move, move!"

For an instant they just stared at her—Wesley and Fred and Angel, and even the demon-draped man who was about to go home to perform the bizarre rituals of a nature so personal that neither Wes nor the man would confess just what they included. Then they parted before her, leaving a clear path to the nearest roundchair. She might be about to lose all control of her limbs, but she'd learned from experience to at least *try* to aim herself at something soft.

A blue demon—a huge gray demon—a small maroon demon . . . bloodbloodblood . . . screaming and flashing metal and a suburban no an urban street no the freeway and it went on and on and on until she lost the details and emerged, finally, so dazed that it took many moments to realize she'd somehow made it to the chair but wasn't alone; Fred fanned her anxiously with a folded piece of paper and Wesley supported her from behind and Angel crouched by the chair, watching her face with an unwavering gaze. Even the demon-draped man hovered in the background, looking like he wished he had something to do in this little tableau.

"What happened?" Angel asked, and his quiet voice let her know it hadn't been any more usual on the outside than from the inside.

Dazed, Cordelia said, "That wasn't a vision, that was a . . . a trip to a multiplex, where all the movies were playing in the same place at the same time!"

"What did you see?" Wes asked. He asked it like he always asked it, as if he actually expected an answer.

"Were you not listening?" Cordelia said incredulously. The phone beeped plaintively in the background, begging to be hung up. "All vision, all the time . . . there's no way I can pick them apart."

Fred paused with the paper-fanning. "But how can we stop them from happening if you can't sort them out?"

"Good point," Wesley said.

"I can't deal with more grannies on my conscience. I can't!"

But Angel only looked at her. After a moment, he said, "We can't. Not individually."

Cordelia nodded slowly. "No. We can't. We've got to stop the thing that's triggering all the trouble."

"The false Angel's client," Wesley said. "If we're to believe what he's said about the man and his relative location to all the recent incidents."

"Oh," Cordelia said, "that reminds me. You might want to call him. That was Gunn on the phone—he said David and Lutkin are on the move." She pulled herself into a more upright sitting position, removing herself from Wesley's support and accepting a cracked ceramic mug of water from the demon-draped guy. "He also said the Tuingas are there, running their own stakeout." Wait, that wasn't right. . . . "No . . . he didn't get the chance. I must have seen them."

"I think we can trust that they'll be involved with the evening, however it goes down," Wesley said.

He stood, digging in his pockets, as Fred quietly replaced the phone in its cradle and eased away. Wesley picked it up again and dialed the old rotary, peering at the paper with David Arnnette's number on it. After a moment, he said, "You're on the move. What can you tell us?"

Arnnette's response came in audible protest, the tone conveying what indistinct words could not. Wesley didn't react, other than to wait it out.

"Not happy we sent Gunn to the hotel," Cordelia guessed.

"See me not caring," Angel said. He rose from his crouch and paced over to the weapons cabinet, then paced back to lean against a pillar.

Wesley said, "I don't believe we ever agreed to allow you to dictate terms. We had the hotel watched. Get over it. What's happening now?" He flipped the small note over and began to scribble on the other side, made a few encouraging noises, and then said, "We'll keep in touch," right before he hung up. Then, he just stared down at his notes for a moment.

"Well?" Cordelia finally prodded him. "What's going on?"

"Quite a lot, it seems," Wesley said. He looked up at them. "Turns out Lutkin knows quite a bit more about what's going on than we suspected, even the faux Angel—until now. He's an artifacts dealer; he's going to make a sale tonight."

"In other words, he's got what the Tuingas want, all right," Fred said. "But . . . not for much longer."

"That's what it looks like," Wesley agreed. "He's still not giving Arnnette any real details—except he's making the exchange at the zoo, where the odors will confuse any Tuingas who are tracking them."

"The zoo's closed," Cordelia observed.

"I imagine that's the least of his worries." Wesley gave the paper a thoughtful tap. "The buy is going down at midnight. We've got to get there before then."

Cordelia glanced at her watch. "Unless you suddenly own Chitty-chitty-bang-bang, I don't think we're going to make it."

"Doesn't matter," Angel said shortly. He flipped a war dart into the air, and caught it. "We'll track down whoever buys it."

"I'm not sure we have that luxury," Wesley said, eyeing Angel closely as he added, "Things seem to be building to an intolerable level. And we just don't know enough about the artifact in question to take such chances."

"Hold on a moment," Cordelia said, rising from the roundchair with a sudden spark of intent that overrode the vision weariness if not the enthusiastic thumping in her head. "Right before Gunn called, I was looking at that weird new book of yours. . . ."

Silence followed her back behind the front counter to the desk, where she found the book on the floor. Smoothing the pages under Wesley's frowning gaze, she found the spot she'd stumbled across just before the phone rang. "There's this one clan of the Tuingas that no one knows much about—I guess they spend most of their time in some pocket dimension. Hmm. Sounds linty."

"I have to say I haven't been able to dig up anything on any Tuingas clan that directly matches what we've seen," Wesley admitted, apparently willing to forgive—or to at least temporarily forget—that she'd damaged his book. "It makes sense that we're dealing with an obscure clan. One that spends most of its time in a pocket dimension, as well. Lorne mentioned that possibility."

"Wait, it gets better." She turned the page, running her finger down the small print on the right-hand side of the page. On the left side of the page was a column containing a map of sightings, a few key symbols indicating demon behavior and habitat—a flexed biceps for strength, blunt teeth showing that they didn't prey on humans but ate vegetable matter, a close-up of a human nose to show they had an extraordinary sense of smell, and a row of five dots with the middle dot in red, showing they were of medium size, at least in demon terms. And at the bottom, the thing that had first caught her attention: the mystical rune symbol the book used to indicate the use of problematic magic—in this case, printed in a cool blue color that meant the problem was coincidental and not deliberate. "Here," she said. "'This robust but rarely observed demon defends itself from food predators by undergoing a lysosomic self-destruction upon death, thus poisoning its own tissues.'"

"It *what?*" the demon-draped man asked blankly.

Cordelia glanced up at him with her *you're still here?* expression as Wesley muttered, "It instantly turns into an excruciatingly smelly goo."

"That *happens?*" The man gave his own demon hitchhiker a look that could have been either wary or hopeful.

"Not in your case, but if you follow the directions I gave you, you should be free of your unwanted guest. Just be sure you don't miss any orifices."

Orifices? Cordelia didn't even want to know. She cleared her throat—loudly—and said, "Short on time here, yes? So here's the thing: Because the demon goes gooey, the other clan members have nothing to remember it by. So they've got this thing called a deathstone that they carry around all the time, and when they die, the stone takes an impression of their psychic emissions at the moment of their death. The other demons go to visit the deathstone like we go to visit a grave site."

Angel tapped the war dart against his palm like he might fiddle with a pencil, his concentration elsewhere. "Not sure this is getting us anywhere," he said. "Getting in the car and going might be a good thing here."

"Do you want to know what we're up against or not?" Cordelia said sharply, giving him a special look from beneath lowered brows—one that reminded him they weren't going to take any guff just because the air was full of bad demon vibes. She ran her finger down the page and found where she'd left off. "Now this is really the thing. These stones are attended by, well . . . priests. And they have to be kept in special environments in these pocket dimensions. Shrines of some sort that protect the stone *and* the demons, because otherwise the stone becomes unstable, and it hits the demons—*any* demon except those Tuingas priests—with the same vibes it absorbed at its demon's death. So, you know—if you have someone who died peacefully, it's not such a huge thing to get under control, but if you've got the deathstone of a Tuingas that was really pissed off when it died, you've got—"

"Trouble," Wes finished for her, looking grim. "And it's quite obviously getting worse over time."

Cordelia put the book aside and raised an eyebrow at her audience. Fred, demon-draped man, Wesley, and—still playing with the war dart

215

with an almost disturbing intensity—Angel. "What do you wanna bet that *gimme* means 'gimme that deathstone'?"

They absorbed the notion in a disturbed silence.

"That's what that ugly stone was," Wes said abruptly. "The one they took back. They were trying to *protect* us."

"And the stone," Angel added. "From their point of view, the stone is probably just as important—if not more."

"I'll bet they were priests," Fred said suddenly.

"What?" they said as one, turning to look at her.

She shrank a little under the combined scrutiny, but stuck it out. "The ones who have come after it, like the one I saw. Their priests aren't affected by the stone, right? So who else would the Tuingas send?"

"Priests," Wesley said slowly. "We've been killing priests."

"*I've* been killing priests," Angel corrected evenly. "And just because you stamp a title on something doesn't mean it's a good something."

Wesley shook his head. "Nonetheless, these particular creatures have been trying to do good. They're trying to recover the very thing that's causing havoc in this city. And they're not overeager to cause incidental damage—several times we ourselves have observed one of them backing away from an unnecessary fight."

"According to my IMAX visions, the havoc we've seen so far is nothing compared with what we *will* see," Cordelia pointed out. "Especially if we don't make it to the zoo on time and have to start tracking this stone all over again."

Their faces reflected bleak understanding; the demon-draped guy gave his living cloak a worried poke. "Maybe I'll try that bar you mentioned," he said.

"Caritas?" Wesley responded absently. "That's not a bad thought. I've no idea what your parasite might do under duress from deathstone emanations, and the spell on Caritas should keep you safe enough. When this is over, though, do come back and let us know how it goes with the . . . eviction."

But Cordelia was barely listening, and barely paid attention to the demon-draped man's departure. Instead she stared at Angel's hand, from which dark blood dripped. He didn't even seem to realize it; he still tapped the dart against his palm, his expression distracted. Elsewhere. "Angel," she said, and then, *"Angel,"* until he looked first at her and then followed her gaze to his hand and to the small dark puddle at his feet.

And then he only shrugged. "I've been known to run with scissors, too."

"That's not funny," Cordelia said. She came around the front counter, taking his hand to look more closely at it, at the multiple glancing puncture wounds he hadn't even appeared to notice. Most of the wounds still welled freely with new blood, but the older ones were already starting to close. "Look at this! What is your problem?"

He held her gaze evenly. "I think you know the answer to that."

"No," she said, "I don't. I mean, I do, but why—"

"—are we wasting time here when we need to get in the car and go?" he said, giving her that look that meant *drop it*. "Before we lose all chance at recovering this thing?"

"But—"

"It was an accident," he snarled, pulling his hand away.

Wesley eyed them both in warning. "*Later*," he said. "For now . . . Angel's right: We need to get our hands on this deathstone. The question is, what exactly will we do when we get it?"

CHAPTER TWELVE

"Just get us going north on the Golden State Freeway," Cordelia said, pointing vaguely over Angel's shoulder from the backseat of the GTX. "The zoo's up that way somewhere, I'm sure of it. Anyway, these things always have signs once you get close, don't they? For all the tourists?"

"For all the people who live in L.A. and never go there," Wesley said from the back seat. "The tourists have maps."

"I know where it is," Angel said shortly. In Wesley's voice he'd heard the same concern now crossing his own mind . . . they weren't going to make it in time. It was a troubled night in a troubled city, and the sound of sirens filled the background. Cars slowed around them, hesitant not because of heavy traffic but because of the strange things the drivers saw . . . or thought they saw . . . or hoped they weren't seeing.

He clenched his hand around the steering wheel, leaving blood. It hurt. But it was a small hurt, and it seemed to help keep his mind clear, just as it had done in the lobby. It was an accident, he'd said . . . and it had been. *Careless distraction with sharp weapons* . . . and enough pain to break through his deathstone-driven agitation.

Not to mention embarrassment when Cordelia was the first of them to realize what he'd done.

Self-consciously, he released his knuckle-cracking grip on the wheel. "Did you reach the fake me yet?"

"It's just been ringing," she said, flipping open her small cell phone to punch the redial. "No, wait"—she glanced at him, success lighting her features— "David, is that you? This is Cordelia. Yeah, you know, from the *real* Angel Investigations. No kidding, we're a little busy too. And we need you to stall. Things are looking bad here and—" She listened a moment, then pulled the phone away from her mouth to push short windblown hair from her eyes and hold it back against her head. "They've hit a snag," she reported to the real Angel Investigations. "They're on their way through Elysian Park—I guess it's pretty rough. The taxi driver abandoned them to hole up at the police academy."

"But that's good," Wes said. "It takes the driver out of the equation. We don't need any more innocents involved here. I'm not sure how it slows them down, though. Surely one of them knows how to drive."

"I said the taxi driver abandoned them. I didn't say he made it far." Cordelia held the phone away from her ear with a sudden wince. "I think they're trying to bash out the divider between the front and the back so they can get to the driver's seat without leaving the car."

Angel took his eyes off the chaotic street—cars suddenly diving for the edge of the road, trying to avoid whatever startling thing they'd come upon, demons scuffling with one another on the center line, fender benders galore—long enough to glance at Cordelia, to see how seriously she was taking the faux Angel's predicament.

Pretty seriously.

"Stay in the car, then!" she was saying. "We're headed that way. We'll scoop you up if we have to—"

And all for the better—they'd have the stone, the carrier, the faux Angel . . . all one tidy little package. From the back, Wesley caught the implications as well, leaning forward over the front seat to listen as he watched Cordelia's expression.

Even from the corner of Angel's eye, using preternatural reflexes to swerve around a small blot of angry something in the road, he could see her wince a second time. "Yeah, okay," she said. "Just stall him as much as you can." And she closed the phone. "That would have been too easy, I guess. Lutkin made a break for it, got behind the wheel. He's still got to get back on the freeway, though— sounds like the taxi driver headed them up Academy Drive before he went all car-aphobic on them."

"Did Lutkin know Arnnette was on the phone with us?" Wes asked, fretting out loud. "It may well have been what spurred him to take such a risk—"

"He took the risk for the same reason he has the deathstone in the first place," Angel said, finding the anger a little too easily. He clamped down on the steering wheel. *Ow.* That was better. *Almost healed, there, but still enough of a sting to—*

"Because he's a greedy old so-and-so," Cordelia said. "He and Arnnette make quite the team, if you ask me."

"I'm guessing he wouldn't care if he did know we were following," Angel said, spotting a clear path in the traffic and accelerating to take it in a few startling swoops of lane changes. "He's ahead of us, and he knows exactly what we're facing. He's in pretty good shape."

"Try Gunn," Wesley suggested. "Maybe he can make better time than we are."

"Trying Gunn," Cordelia said, activating the phone again. "Let's hope his luck is better than ours."

• • •

Get to the zoo, Cordelia had told him. *Get there now.*

Gunn stared at his cell phone, then flipped it closed.

"Let us come along," Sinthea said, eavesdropping with intent and then pouncing.

He immediately struck out for the truck, trying to absorb all that Cordelia had babbled at him. "I need you here," he said. "It's a bad night. You need to cover your own streets, not—"

"—join you where all the action is?" Tyree finished for him.

Gunn mustered his patience. "Stray from your turf. This is way up at the zoo. Besides, this isn't the kind of action you're looking for. Our guy's got something; we're going to keep him from selling it to another guy. Mostly in between we've got traffic jams." He didn't mention the demons going wild along the way that were causing the traffic jams. These kids weren't ready to go into a situation where Gunn couldn't protect their backs . . . and no matter what they thought, they wouldn't be ready until they were willing to listen to him.

"Sounds to me like you're cutting us out," Sinthea said.

"Does it?" Gunn said, turning on them and letting his voice go hard. The truck sat only half a block away; the zoo was much farther. Time grew absurdly short. "I can't imagine why I'd do that, can you? Why I'd go out on *my* business without letting you in on every piece of it."

"You cut us in on watching the hotel," Tyree said, giving Gunn a cold stare even the night couldn't hide. "We were good enough for that."

Gunn could be cold, too. And neither Tyree nor his following were of any use to him—or themselves—if they were going to fight him all the way. "You couldn't be just a little bit like the fake Angel?" he muttered to himself, leaving the two teens exchanging a puzzled glance. Louder, he said, "It's not gonna happen. And the more grief you give me, the more I'm sure it's not gonna happen. You catch my meaning on that?"

"Tsk, tsk," said the man who was suddenly leaning against the tailgate to Gunn's truck. He had a fluffy Afro that needed picking, and wore low-slung bell-bottoms below a brightly patterned polyester shirt. He didn't quite have his fangs showing. "It's not going to happen, all right—but not for the reasons you think."

"Hey," Gunn said, offended, and automatically cataloguing the weapons and potential weapons on his person. Not a lot. More in the truck. *Of course.* "Get your grave-clammy little hands off my truck."

"Why's that? You need it? You trying to get

somewhere? You should have paid better attention. And really, you should know better than to hang around this part of town."

Gunn snorted. "You must be new here. This is *my* part of town."

"And mine," Sinthea said boldly, stepping up beside Gunn.

As far as he knew, she hadn't come out with anything sharp and wooden hidden in the revealing outfit he'd already noted.

"And mine," Tyree agreed, looking at the vampire through half-lidded eyes with a lazily threatening expression that would scare the pants off anything human.

This not being a human, it just got a wider smile. "You know," the vampire said, "I've been in this really bad mood all day, but for some reason it just got much better."

"I don't have time for this," Gunn said, exasperated. A quick check showed the vamp to be alone, but—"Watch my back," he said to the kids, and moved in, the stake from his back pocket already in his hand.

"Oh goody, it's dinner entertainment," the vamp said, and he stood back from the truck slightly. Then, giving Gunn a sly look, he very deliberately kicked the fender.

Gunn slowly shook his head. "That was such a bad move."

Which was when Tyree grabbed the stake from Gunn's hand and rushed the vampire, plowing into him so they both bounced off the truck, and plunging the stake into the vamp's chest with all his considerable strength. He leaped away, his expression pure I-told-you-so in Gunn's direction.

"Nice," Gunn said, crossing his arms to watch the vamp as he clung to the side of the truck, imminent death in his expression. "One little problem there. Or two."

Tyree frowned slightly. "Shouldn't he be—?"

"Yeah. Except you missed his heart."

The significance of this fact eased through Tyree's thoughts and made it all the way to his face as the vamp gave a little smile, tugged the stake out, and threw it far down the street.

Implacably, Gunn said, "The other problem being you gave away my best stake to do it."

From behind them, Sinthea said, "And then there's that third problem." Her steady voice gave away nothing of her fear, but her meaning was clear enough: *Our vamp didn't come alone after all*. Which was why he'd told them to watch. They hadn't, and now he'd lost his best weapon and two girly vamps in really low hip-hugging bell-bottoms and halter tops had their hands on Sinthea. They had vamp faces turned on full and nasty expressions that meant Sinthea was only alive because they felt like playing with their food.

And it wasn't like the distance to the zoo was getting any shorter while he stood here. He threw his hands up and made a noise of disgust. "Don't have time for this," he warned the vampires, reaching for a backup stake, one that had broken in the last fight and wasn't quite long enough. "You wanna skip to the end and stake yourselves for us?"

For some reason they thought that was funny. Gunn shrugged. He tossed the stake to Tyree and said, "Don't do anything fancy. Stick to defense. I'll be there in a moment." And from the cargo pocket of his jeans he withdrew the black lacquered chopsticks he'd grabbed from Wesley's desk just because it seemed to be his turn—and also, he had to admit, because he'd seen the potential to needle Angel.

Tyree just stared at the chopsticks, and then at the stake in his hand. Gunn snapped, "Do it! Defense!" And he turned to the first vampire and said, "I believe I told you to get away from that truck."

"And I believe I laughed," the vampire said.

No time for this.

Gunn attacked. A chopstick in either hand, well-protected within his fist, he went in with his brutally efficient style, going for confusion instead of the straight kill Tyree had led the vampire to expect. Body blows, a few jabs to the nose, the crunch of separating cartilage and bone . . . as the vampire reeled back, astonishment on his face, Gunn wheeled around, checked his angle—the chopstick had to go in perfectly straight, sliding upward through ribs into heart or it would break before it even approached its target—and slammed the chopstick home.

The vamp's astonishment made way for dust as Gunn snarled, "I told you—*not* the truck!" and then whirled on the two teens and the hippie vamps.

Tyree had freed Sinthea, and they stood back-to-back, finally doing just what they'd been told: keeping the hippie vamps at bay and nothing more. *Barely* keeping them at bay, for both of them bled, and Sinthea had that dazed look and a mousing eye; she'd taken some hits. The vamps were doing just what they'd wanted: playing with the food.

Until Gunn, with perfect timing, planted a heavy kick in the middle of the closer one's back, a shove-kick that impaled the vampire on Tyree's borrowed stake. There was no aim to it, and the hippie vampire shrieked but didn't dust off—but this time, Tyree immediately realized the situation, withdrew the stake, and slammed it home again.

The final vampire hesitated, just the merest instant in recognition of the changed odds, and Sinthea cried, "*My* neighborhood," and fell on her in a fury. It couldn't last; no normal human could outlast a vampire that way. But Tyree threw Gunn the stake, and Gunn jumped in behind the vampire as she staggered back; as she looked up at him in surprise, he brought his arms around her in a false embrace from behind and neatly dusted her, careful not to use so much force that the stake ended up in his own chest as well.

Tyree grabbed Sinthea just in time to keep her from folding to the ground, giving her the moment's support she needed before she could stand on her own again—which she did, moving away from him to prove it. Gunn said shortly, "Get the stake he threw down the street. Keep it with you tonight, but your job is to spot them"—vampires, demons, sewer creature mutts—"and keep everyone else away from them, *not* kill them. Unless you want to risk losing your life to something that can only be killed by an eagle feather dipped in mercury and stabbed into its eye while you think you can kill it with a blade."

"There's something like that out there . . . ?" Sinthea asked, still breathing heavily—though her hand, as she tucked her hair behind her ear, was as steady as Gunn could have hoped for.

"Until you don't have to ask, you'll just have to trust me," he said.

This time, she barely hesitated. She nodded, and she didn't say whatever impulse of protest lurked behind the quick tightening of her lips.

He tossed her the short stake, and tucked the chopsticks back in his pocket. In an unconscious instant of imitation, Sinthea did the same with the stake.

Gunn hid the small smile that tugged at his mouth, and headed for his truck. "Call if you need help," he said, and for the first time he thought they probably would.

It occurred to him as he climbed in the truck that he had no intention of revealing what the chopsticks had been through before he replaced them on Wesley's desk.

CHAPTER THIRTEEN

"**I**'m thinking I hope Gunn goes another way." Cordelia looked out over the chaos of the Golden State Freeway. The dark trees of Elysian Park lined the southwest side of the freeway . . . as did too many cars to count. It had turned into a group experience, this pulling over to the far lane to stop and say *Did you see that?* to people you didn't know . . . people who on another evening would honk and shout and make rude gestures but on this day merely contributed to the mess.

Although, of course, the honkers and shouters were out in force as well.

"Take heart," Wesley said, raising his voice. "Lutkin and the faux Angel had to come this way too. Even if they made it off Academy Drive to the Pasadena Freeway ahead of us, they can't be too far ahead. Not in this."

● ● ●

Demon blood turned the streets red.

And orange, and sticky green, and one color Gunn didn't care to describe.

He drove up Alvarado, eyeing pavement that looked like a paintball battle had taken place—and knowing that most people would believe that to be the case. Gunn himself only truly understood since Cordy's quick phone data dump. *What a mess.* He'd already rolled over one demon himself. It had been so enraged by the deathstone emanations that it had apparently been unable to perceive the basic flaw in playing chicken with a full-sized pickup truck, and Gunn doubted it would have any opportunity to apply its new knowledge to future encounters. It had, if he recalled correctly, bled yellow, an ugly stain under the streetlights as seen in his rearview mirror.

He switched the radio on, tuning to KFWB—"All News, All the Time." Not his usual fare, but they had good traffic reports—*as if anyone could keep up with this*—and, given the circumstances . . . still, jabber jabber jabber. . . . He turned the radio down and concentrated on making time, not the least bit concerned that the overworked cops would tag him for speeding.

They were already plenty busy tonight. Mostly getting there too late, puzzling over the inexplicable aftermath of a drive-by demoning, trying to take reports, comfort witnesses, grab up the still-living and get them to medical help. Gunn passed a handful of stopped patrol cars with flashers going and muttered, "Give it up, guys. You're in *waaay* over your head."

He wondered if the same might not be said of him.

Here he was, racing to help someone who not so long ago had made an aborted attempt to kill him. He could have stayed where he was, supervising the youthful and barely prepared neighborhood watch. He could have gone back to his gang—they didn't pretend to understand his new focus with Angel Investigations, but then again, sometimes neither did he. And they would have welcomed the extra hands on a night like this, along with the wealth of experience on which he could draw.

Extra hands. Maybe that's what it came down to. Honorable as it was, he didn't want to fight these battles as a foot soldier. He didn't want to be an extra hand. He wanted to be in the center of the action, making a difference. He'd understood from the start that it meant working with Angel, and he'd adjusted to that fact.

But every now and then something happened to remind him just who Angel was. Just *what* he was.

And just what lurked within him.

But the bottom line remained the same: He wanted to be in the center of it all, combating L.A.'s problems at the source. He wanted to be at

the zoo tonight, and not prowling the streets ignorant of the larger picture. And it still meant working with Angel.

So yes, here he was, racing to help someone who
not so long ago had made an aborted attempt to
kill him. Because when it came down to it, he was
racing to help everyone under siege in L.A.

"Aim high," he muttered to himself. Though he
couldn't let the dry amusement distract him from
another bottom line . . . that the phrase *know thy
enemy* sometimes potentially applied to Angel.

Tonight—in a violence-riddled city inundated
with deathstone emanations that also targeted
Angel—held more potential for it than most.

So. Don't forget it . . .

He took the entrance ramp from Allesandro to the
Golden State fast enough to make the outside
wheels taste air, checking behind him to see that
he'd come in ahead of the big, slow glob of head-
lights . . . the area beside Elysian Park, where the
trees crowded the freeway and who-knows-what
could come crawling up the steep park slope.
Wouldn't even have to be a violent who-knows-
what—just something driven out of hiding; the way
people rubbernecked at the simplest fender bender,
a single exposed demon could snarl traffic for miles.

Gunn was betting there'd been more than one.

" . . . zoo," said the radio broadcaster, a puzzled
note in his voice—as if he wasn't sure why he was

reading puff headlines in the middle of demon wars, no doubt already being labeled gang activity of some bizarre sort. "The Aussie Auction fund-raiser is being held in Koala Corner, where many of the creatures from Down Under will be available for viewing, some of them up close and personal. This invitation-only auction is limited to three hundred people, all of whom will be bringing their checkbooks. . . ."

Great. Big do at the zoo. Innocent, clueless civilians, with no idea of the crisis that darkness and an unstable deathstone had wrought. And Lutkin creeping around in the dark, with his own personal fund-raiser in motion.

Angel gave the parking lot a baffled glance. The zoo should be long closed, the lot empty, the gates locked.

"We're going to have a hard time finding Lutkin in this," Cordelia observed with disapproval, her mouth curled down on one side to match her tone of voice.

"Hell, we're going to have a hard time finding Gunn in this," Angel said, cruising slowly between rows of parked cars, fighting the impulse to jam his foot on the accelerator and zoom through the rows at the kind of speed his reflexes could handle. Fast, tire-squealing, hair-raising speed that would fulfill some dark corner of his—

Not his. Just feedback from the stone they were here to liberate.

In the next row over, several people disembarked from a zoo tram, after which the tram slowly puttered back toward the entrance and eased to a stop. "They're starting to leave," Wesley said. "We should hurry. This may be our best way into the zoo."

"*What* might be our best way in?" Cordelia asked, looking a little wary.

Wesley waved a vague hand at the parking lot, at the leaving visitors. "This," he said.

The man and woman walking to their silver Lexus wore formal evening attire, chic without being overdressed, expensive without being gaudy. Angel looked down at himself. Black leather jacket, black leather pants. Black T-shirt—or at least a black Pima cotton pullover that pretended to be more than a T-shirt but really wasn't. Stark and unadorned. Wesley had a three-button henley over slacks, and Cordelia— looking great as usual—wore a totally funky halter top under a hooded knit jacket and over low-slung jeans, and carried a big canvas weapons bag. "We aren't exactly going to blend in."

"And we shouldn't try," Wesley replied. Then, startled, he pointed out to the empty end of the parking lot. "Is that—?"

Angel let the car idle, following Wesley's gesture.

Gunn. Standing atop his pickup truck. Not in the truck bed, but on top of the cab itself. Also not blending in. When he spotted them spotting him, he waved in an arm-crossing signal flag gesture and hopped down from the truck.

With a glance at the gate, Angel reluctantly drove to the open area, parking alongside Gunn.

Gunn didn't even wait for them to pile out of the car. "Did you spot them? I haven't seen them— which is just a little strange, considering they were in a taxi."

Angel surveyed a parking lot full of sleek cars in sleek colors as they gathered between the vehicles. Nothing so obvious or garish as a taxi service sign sitting on the roof of any of them. "This is where he said they were coming."

"It's close to midnight," Wesley observed. "Even if they made it here ahead of us, they should be in there somewhere. And I think it's reasonable to assume that the traffic obstacles and the situation here has slowed them down."

"Aussie Auction," said Gunn.

Cordelia said, "What's that? And what does it have to do with finding the deathstone?"

"It's a big moneymaking deal in Koala Corner, wherever that is. And it's in our way. Invitation only, so we can't just pretend we're with the program."

"Not at all," Wesley said with satisfaction. "The people from the tram are leaving the event, which must be just about over. And people who're leaving aren't nearly as careful with their invitations as people who are entering. This could well be much easier than trying to get in when the zoo is otherwise empty."

Cordelia sighed. "Search the parking lot?"

"More than that," Angel said. "Watch the people coming out. If Lutkin made it in there, so did the fake Angel . . . and so did Lutkin's buyer. Even if we didn't get here in time to stop the buy, they've all got to come back out."

"Divide and conquer," Wesley said. "Angel, your night vision would serve us best if you act as lookout in case they *do* come back out. The rest of us will take a quick look for dropped invitations—not to mention that taxi. It would be nice to have confirmation that they were here at all."

Angel opened his mouth . . . closed it again. Wesley was in charge now. That's the way it had to be for the gang to deal with their recent conflict . . . *his* recent behavior as he tried to deal with Darla's presence and what she and Wolfram and Hart had planned for him. That's the way it had been since they'd come together again. Why it should raise such resentment at this point, such an intense impulse to go fang-face and—

Because of the bad mojo, to quote a certain Host.

He suddenly realized the others had hesitated, were watching him, doubt and suspicion on their faces. That his every thought had probably been reflected on his face.

On the other hand, there was the night vision thing. Maybe they were just waiting for him to say something stunningly wise.

Or not.

"Okay," he said simply, and headed for a vantage point closer to the pennant-lined walkway that led to the round, modular entrance gate, well aware that he'd both surprised them and that they weren't entirely satisfied by the exchange. He stood in a pool of shadow, taking up his post unseen by the tram driver as the woman finished her coffee break, stuffed a thermos in the pouch beside her seat, and put the tram back in motion. Even as she entered the zoo, several patrons exited, on foot and cheery in their conversation. They probably didn't even know there was a vampire lurking within striking distance, and wouldn't have had the faintest idea what to do if—

Stop that.

Bad vampire. Bad. Count to ten, ignore the pulse and swell of someone else's emotion battering him from the outside in. Watch for Lutkin and a version of Angel who really didn't look anything like him at all and, above all, keep control of that part within that felt such kinship with the dark emotions of this night and ceaselessly battered at him from the inside out. *Angelus.*

"Get lost," he muttered to that part of himself.

He thought he heard the faint sound of laughter.

Cordelia immediately found the halves of an invitation, figured it would look torn in half and unconvincing no matter what she did with it, and tucked the halves into her pocket to throw away later. "Really," she said out loud. "Some people are such pigs." *Ripping up a perfectly good invitation like that . . .*

She heard voices, and ducked down between cars, staring steadfastly at the ground to make herself feel invisible. There was no point in trying to look casual in this parking lot, underdressed as she was and lurking as she so obviously was. So of course the voices drew closer, and closer, and . . . stopped.

With much trepidation, she surreptitiously peered upward. An exquisitely dressed man and his exquisitely dressed male escort looked down at her, extreme disapproval and suspicion not the least bit hidden on their faces. "Honey," Cordelia said loudly, "did you find it yet?"

From the next row over and coming closer, Gunn said, "What are you—," and then switched gears so obviously that Cordelia wanted to smack her own forehead. "No, dear, still looking." Where'd he learn his delivery, from watching *Leave It to Beaver* reruns? *Whatever*. She was the actress here; she'd have to save the scene.

She allowed herself to discover the couple. "Oh—hi! This must be your car. Nice car. I lost a ring around here somewhere earlier today. . . ." She moved out of the way so one of the men could open the front passenger door, and they eyed her with identical, barely mollified expressions, interrupting only to eye Gunn with the very same doubt.

She smiled like someone preoccupied with finding a ring and thought she'd carried it off quite well, too, until the fellow getting into the car muttered at her, "A flashlight might have helped."

"Dead batteries," she chirped ruefully, trying to keep her eye-rolling expression from manifesting itself. She returned to looking under cars as they watched, exchanging words within the car until she thought they were going to change their minds and find someone to report her to. Finally the driver started the engine and slowly backed out of the parking spot. Cordelia heaved a sigh of relief, snatched up the invitation the driver had dropped when he fished out his car key, and went to join Gunn. "Boy, did that suck. I thought they were going to . . . ," but she trailed off, for he was paying no attention whatsoever. Stung, she squelched an impulse to skewer his Ward Cleaver imitation and instead followed his gaze.

The taxi. Checker Cab, located right on Alvarado, along with the Alvarado Palms Hotel, where Lutkin had made his temporary home. *The sign had been torn off the roof—deliberately,* Cordelia thought, so the car wouldn't stand out in the parking lot. As if it weren't covered with deep claw scratches, unidentifiable goo, and distinct tooth marks. And as if it weren't yellow and several years old, unlike any other car in the lot.

"So they *are* here," Wesley said, coming up to join them.

"Unless they snuck out past Angel since we got here," Gunn said.

Wesley glanced back toward the entry walk. "In his present mood, I'm thinking that's not likely. He's rather . . . alert."

"He'll be okay," Cordelia said, mostly because someone had to say it. She held out her scavenged invitation. "Here's one that'll get two of us in."

Wesley gave a short shake of his head. "Forget the invitations."

"After what I just went through—?"

"*Because* of what you just went through. We were lucky—those two were obviously suspicious, and might just as well have chosen to cause trouble for us. And there will be more people leaving the auction with every passing moment. No, it was a good idea, but I think we'll have to try something else."

"Like?" Gunn said, with the challenging tone of someone who doesn't expect there to be an answer.

"Like a more straightforward bluff." Wesley

headed for the nook where Cordelia had last seen Angel lurking. She couldn't see him now, of course, not when he had no intention of being seen. Where a human would have been drawn out of the shadows in order to see those he observed, Angel could see just fine from whatever dark corner he chose.

He came out to meet them, his head cocked at the zoo entry in such a way to make it obvious he was listening—that the tram was on its way back out. "Any particular straightforward bluff?" he asked, having of course heard that as well, along with any comment made about his present mood. Cordelia would have blushed if she hadn't been distracted by circumstances. Or if she'd cared what he heard. That was the nice thing about speaking your mind: When you did it out of habit, the things you said behind someone's back were simply the very same things you'd say to their face.

"This one," Wes said as the tram hummed along out of the zoo and stopped to disgorge several couples. He strode for the tram like one who'd been waiting impatiently all along, leaving the others to rush to catch up. Cordelia arrived at the vehicle's broad step-up in time to hear the woman driver say in a bored sort of voice, "Zoo's closed, buddy. And I don't even have a change purse."

"We're here to break down the event lighting," Wesley said. "The Burns Foundation sent us along . . . a last-minute gesture."

Cordelia inwardly raised an eyebrow, impressed. On the exterior she contrived to look like someone who might know how to break down event lighting. No doubt it involved unplugging. She could fake it if she had to.

Though she doubted Wesley meant for things to go that far.

The woman shrugged, flipping a thin, straw-blond ponytail back over her shoulder with an absent gesture. She nodded at the clipboard jammed into the holder beside the steering column, a move she surely wouldn't make if she knew how many chins it gave her. "No one said anything about it to me."

"I hate it when that happens," Gunn said, though it was more like the growl of someone who just wanted to pull the driver out of her seat, take over control, and drive on into the zoo to ditch the vehicle and find the bad guys. Or at least, find the deathstone.

Wesley gave him an entirely ineffective glare. "Yes," he said, "annoying, isn't it? I had a ball game planned with my son, and then the phone rang, and . . ." He shrugged.

"Well," said the driver, not particularly caring, "you gotta sign off on this sheet, then. And you gotta get out just before we reach Koala Corner, so the tram is empty for the guests."

"Certainly," said Wesley, and he took the

proffered clipboard to scrawl a meaningless signature as they hopped aboard.

"Burns Foundation," Gunn muttered to Wesley as he took his seat and the tram lurched into motion. "Good one. Did you get that from *The Simpsons*?"

"No," Wesley said. "I got it from the zoo newsletter. The foundation is one of their most generous benefactors."

Gunn made an expression of patent surprise that Wesley should know such a thing, but it was bait Wesley didn't rise to with anything more than the smallest lift of an eyebrow. *Just as well*, Cordelia thought. This was serious now. They were here in the zoo at night, with the sounds of the outdoor auction trickling through the night, and glimpses of the festive lighting as the tram moved along the curvy pathway. The open-air design of the tram made it easy to take in the dark grounds they hummed through. Though all the animals were in for the night, the late hour and the essentially abandoned state of the grounds somehow made the place all the more theirs, turning Cordelia and Wesley and Angel and Gunn into intruders and the auction itself into a patiently tolerated anomaly. *Snap out of it*, she told herself. *We're here for a reason.*

Because Lutkin was here, and he and his buyer. Because the Tuingas would no doubt be close behind, and not at all concerned with the niceties of getting in the zoo. It occurred to her that the buyer had probably been invited to the auction, and had simply walked right in through the front gate. Perhaps he'd even gained Lutkin's entrance as his guest.

From the corner of her eye, she saw something flit between tree and bush, make a strafing run at the tram, and disappear behind them. "Uh-oh," she said. "We're not the only ones visiting after-hours."

"Yes," Wesley said grimly. "I've seen a thing or two myself. I think we can assume the stone is drawing them."

"The question is, does David Arnnette know that?" Lutkin, she didn't care about. Lutkin had known what he was getting into. Enough to run the other way instead of take the greedy side of the force. But Arnnette, annoying and wrong-headed as he was, hadn't really earned himself center of attention in a monster melee.

"We're going the wrong direction," Angel said abruptly as the tram made a sweeping left turn through the beautifully landscaped area, putting the administration building and shops of the entrance behind them to pass the alligators on one side and a deeply shadowed line of trees on the other. He gazed off to the right with an odd look on his face. A strained look, full of shadow and flickering between anger and determination.

"How do you—," Wesley started, stopping as he glanced over, as if the very sight of Angel was answer enough.

Angel didn't seem to notice. "I can feel it," he said. "Before, it was just here. In the zoo. But now . . . we're going away from it."

"Not far," Gunn said, looking ahead through the framework of the huge glassless tram windows. "If we get off here, we'll have the zoo people hunting for us—"

"If *you* get off here," Angel said. And before Cordelia could cry out, *No, wait,* he was on the seat and out the window, one of those seamless moves that only a man with hundreds of years of familiarity with his body could make.

Cordelia glanced at the driver, who had not surprisingly failed to notice, and closed her mouth. Angel was on his own, now.

At least for a while. She patted the big floppy bag by her side.

It gave her the reassuring clank of metal in return.

CHAPTER FOURTEEN

Angel landed in a crouch, a swirl of leather and the gentle thump of soft soles against manicured ground. The tram moved on, carrying the others away from him for now; as its quiet engine noise faded, other noises moved in. The faint human chatter of the auction . . . restless animals behind closed doors, well aware that this was no normal night at the zoo. Polar bears, seals . . . from across the zoo came the sound of a frustrated tiger, and from another quarter altogether, a lion. Not sounds that wholly human ears could hear.

And there were other noises. Creatures from outside the zoo, having invited themselves in. Demons of various shapes and sizes and intelligence, easing across the zoo grounds, making a wide berth around the noise and light of the Aussie Auction because now, here, their only focus was the stone that tormented them.

Tormented him.

It pulled him, it dragged him . . . it slapped against him in waves of pitched fury that threatened to overwhelm his humanity. He felt himself slipping into fang-face and fought it; his hand, newly healed, did nothing to distract him when he clenched it. The night closed in around him—

"Good evening," said a tux-clad man walking the path from the auction, his date on his arm and his expression jovial and self-assured. He held an auction receipt loosely in one hand like a trophy, and was preoccupied enough with his date that he didn't notice the odd jerk with which Angel looked away.

They smelled good.

They smelled really good.

That's not who you are.

Human. Carrying a soul that already dragged too much guilt around with it, a soul that didn't even need to *know* how hard it was for this body to keep itself from leaping on the unsuspecting couple—supper and dessert rolled into one.

"Good evening," Angel said in a low voice, only through long practice able to keep his words clear around protruding teeth. And if the man thought to give Angel a strange look, he was distracted quickly enough by his date's obsession with the auction receipt, and had no apparent clue that the warring factions within this stranger had in fact been warring over his fate.

That in itself was some small victory, and as they moved on, Angel allowed himself to relax, not entirely sure if he'd won that round or if he'd just—fortunately—run out of time. A new spasm of wholly exterior anger beat against him . . . the deathstone in the throes of overload.

They were *all* running out of time.

Cordelia led the trio as they disembarked from the tram a short distance from the brightly lit and thickly occupied enclave in front of the koala house; by unspoken consent they said nothing of Angel at all, and successfully ignored the little frown on the driver's face. The woman flipped her ponytail back, frowned again at the single scrawled signature Wesley had left her, and shrugged. She eased the tram toward the mouth of Koala Corner, leaving them to follow.

They didn't, of course. They headed back down the pathway, not at all certain where they were going—or how to get there from here. "Gosh," Cordelia said, sardonic as she contemplated an implacable row of trees between them and where she thought Angel had been looking right before he bailed off the bus. "How silly of us. We should have stopped to get a touristy little map on the way in."

"I suggest we head for Treetops Terrace," Wesley said. "It's a focal point of the zoo, and is a likely spot for the exchange. Furthermore, it's high ground. Even if it's not the right place, it's a good spot for reconnaissance."

"Sure," said Cordelia. "If only I'd brought my weekend warrior night-vision goggles."

"If only we still had Angel with us," Gunn said, more than a hint of accusation in his voice.

"Hey, if we're lucky, we'll find the right spot and he'll have already taken care of everything," Cordelia said, trying hard to look on the positive side.

"The state of mind he must be in, I don't think we want him taking care of anything," Wesley told her.

"The state of mind he's in, I'd rather have him here beside us than sneaking up behind us," Gunn added immediately. "Or do I have to remind you—"

"No," Cordelia said sharply. "You don't. Now can we get moving? The only thing worse than sneaking through a dark zoo when you know there are demons lurking all around is hanging around in a dark zoo looking defenseless and yummy." Not that they were defenseless. But she didn't want to have to deal with convincing some deathstone-driven demon that they weren't worth the trouble. After all, how does a deathstone-driven demon measure such things? Quite certainly not on the same scale that Cordelia would use.

A rustle off the side drew all their attention at once; they froze, waiting to see if the unknown creature would pass or come in for a closer look. After a moment it moved on, and Cordelia let out a gusty sigh.

"I hope my kids *listened*," Gunn muttered.

"What?" asked Wesley.

"Nothing," Gunn told him. "Let's get this over with."

A night-shift zoo attendant moved briskly toward the aviary, looking around himself with his shoulders shrugged up—as though the back of his neck prickled . . . or he knew he was being watched.

Angel watched him. At least three demons also watched him. Run-of-the-mill demon-human mutts who probably ordinarily spent their evenings playing poker or racing rats. To the left, the pull of the stone . . . to the right, the defenseless keeper and the chance to give in to the intense and constant itch of emotion.

Act. Attack. Do it in fury.

The demons gave in to the itch—and with an inner leap of dissolved restraint, Angel followed. Faster than the demons, more practiced . . . he got there first. The keeper squeaked in fear at the sudden company, ducking away from Angel.

Angel didn't look at him. He didn't turn to the keeper, he didn't so much as glance at the keeper, and he definitely kept his face in shadow. "Get in the aviary cage," he said, facing the startled demon mutts. "Get in there and stay in there. If you come out, you'll die." *And who knows. It might even be me who kills you.*

An Angelus thought if there ever was one. *I can be angry and still human,* he told that part of himself, a vicious inner dialogue.

He took it out on the demons. They weren't tough demons; they came in with teeth showing, and fists flailing as though to pummel him to submission; one of them had javelina-like tusks that might even do some damage. Angel succumbed to temptation, let loose his iron control, and launched himself at them.

He took them down in a savage combination of moves—breaking what he could have merely bruised, killing where he could have incapacitated. Not killing all of them . . . two looked at their injuries with a kind of shocked revelation—broken nose gushing blood, broken arm jutting bone—and then down at the dead tusk-face as revelation turned to realization. As though suddenly they understood where they were and what they'd been up to and what kind of trouble they were in. And Angel, the back of his hand barely stinging from the dying slash of a tusk, laughed at them.

And then he chased them. Arms open wide, embracing the night and the violence and the death he could cause . . .

Angeluuusss.

A glad whisper in his thoughts. A recognition of self, only moments from freedom . . .

The demons threw themselves over a wall and into the packed dirt pit below. Tires dotted the ground, along with a large squashed plastic barrel. *Elephant enclosure.* Angel stopped, hesitated; considered. One of the demons seemed to have injured its leg. Not much of a chase any longer. And then behind him . . .

The deathstone pulsed his own fierce intensity at him, recapturing him like a siren song of destruction. He turned his back on the elephant enclosure and took his bearings.

A cluster of small hexagonal buildings stood front and left; his night vision was plenty good enough to read the REPTILE HOUSE sign. Almost directly in front of him stood an open area with picnic facilities. ZOO MEADOW. Up the hill to the right, beyond a crescent of palms, stood a fanciful building with a subdued glow of minimal night lighting.

There.

The stone was up there.

Khundarr tightened the flap of his long-nose tightly enough to make it ache. *Faugh,* what a place this was! No matter that it was clean and tidy and manicured . . . there was no mistaking the overlapping scent of so many different animals residing in this one facility.

But there was also no mistaking the presence of the warrior's deathstone. The stone's emissions oscillated and wobbled, more strongly pitched than Khundarr had ever detected in his days as a priest. Strong enough for his new team of under-priests to locate it and emerge from their pocket dimension not far from where Khundarr waited.

As a team, they entered the zoo, not terribly concerned with the bars and rules of human facilities, nor concerned about the consequences. They would be lucky to live out this night and, if by some chance they *did*, escape back to the pocket dimension was the least of their worries.

For the night was full of demons. Demons from deep nooks and crannies of their clandestine lives, drawn out by the irresistible call of a stone so full of impressions that it spiraled toward destruction. It taunted them, inflicting its emanations on them, luring them back to the source. . . .

Khundarr had seen the results. Mild demons, dying in streets they never otherwise dared to visit. Fierce demons, tearing one another apart. And the humans, who never stood a chance either way, entirely unprepared for the attack of those creatures they rarely saw and never acknowledged. Come morning, the chaos would hardly abate, and then the humans would see an entirely new world, revealed in bright daylight. Only those wretches who hid in the darkest corners of their homes would be able to deny the existence of the demon element . . . and that would mean the start of an entirely different kind of war—and an end to the uneasy, covert coexistence of the elder ones and the humans who had displaced them.

Not to mention the astonishing numbers of both humans and demons who would die before the deathstone finally imploded with the weight of its own impressions.

Unless Khundarr and his team regained possession of the deathstone. Here. Now. At this place where two foolish humans seemed to think that the distasteful smell of carefully collected animals could throw the Tuingas from the trail of the deathstone, a thing they perceived through an entirely different sense altogether. Where those humans thought they could barter the power of a warrior's deathstone without consequence.

Khundarr intended to create consequence.

"No wonder they picked the zoo," Gunn said, even as Cordelia caught a musky whiff of some creature or another. Or maybe just a combination of all of them. "Even with the way they clean this place, the smell—"

"Should prove confusing to any scent-oriented

creature like the Tuingas," Wesley agreed. "But ultimately, I doubt it'll be enough. Angel seems to know where the stone is—"

"And he's not the only one," Cordelia interrupted, moving a few quick inches closer to the two of them as something rustled in the landscaped brush behind her. Not a big something, since that particular brush wasn't even up to her knees. But *something* nonetheless. "Where's this Treetops place you were talking about—oh." For they'd found the paved path again, and it curved immediately uphill and to the left, where on the high ground, a fanciful building that looked like two hexagons crammed together gently glowed with soft night lighting around what looked like giant aquariums set into the walls. The roof rose up at a steep hut-like angle, and Cordelia wasn't sure if they were walking into a scene from *The Little Mermaid* or Tarzan's condo.

Or maybe just some dirty little sale of stolen goods . . . a deathstone for cash.

The buyer stood off to the side, barely limned by the soft blue light of the aquarium walls. He'd either been at the auction or dressed for it as a matter of course; his suit looked Italian and most definitely hand-tailored by someone with enough skill to disguise—almost—the long-bodied and short-legged build of the man, not to mention his mild paunch.

Lutkin's taste in clothing had not changed a whit—not for the occasion and not out of mercy for the rest of them. And in his hand . . . the bowling bag. At his back stood David Arnnette, glancing into the darkness with an increasing nervousness.

A nearby growl startled Cordelia. More startling yet, it was a familiar kind of growl, and how often did you get to say that? She found . . .

Angel.

He'd been in a fight already, had a scuff of blood on his face from a wound that had already healed—or might not have been his in the first place. And his face itself . . . tense, and shadowed from within. Not quite fang-face, but looking on the verge . . . tormented and yet in some way eager, a scary combination. She wasn't even sure—

"Angel?" Wesley asked quietly.

"It's me," Angel said, short and with just a hint of dark humor. "Trust me. If Angelus was in control, I wouldn't just be watching."

"Trust you, *no*," Gunn said. "But the logic works."

"There it is," Wesley said, his attention on the exchange before them. The buyer extended a briefcase; Arnnette fielded it and gave the contents a token look before setting the case by Lutkin's side with a quick, nervous movement that suggested he wanted nothing to do with the money or the situation. He glanced around, peering through the darkness as though he wished he indeed had a vampire's night vision, all the more conspicuous in his effort to look casual.

Looking for us, Cordelia realized. Hoping *for us.* Finally realizing he was in over his head. Though in this case she wasn't sure if "better late than never" applied, because maybe—for Arnnette, for the Tuingas, for all the people hurt by enraged demons, for *Angel*—maybe late was simply too late.

Khundarr hovered at the edge of the odd building, with eyes for nothing but the undignified bag that held the warrior's deathstone. Or not quite so; he was not so careless that he didn't note the presence of those from the hotel, although neither the man with the deathstone nor the buyer seemed to know of them. Khundarr's team of priests ranged around the area, circling the exchange and ready for action. Ready to grab the deathstone no matter what it took—for while they had no wish to kill humans, things had gone too far. They would recover the deathstone tonight no matter the cost.

The black human looked around, wary, as though he somehow detected the priests; he murmured something to the other two humans. If Khundarr's team were properly alert, they would note the exchange. If not, they were likely to pay. These humans knew how to fight. But the vampire was the biggest problem, and not only because of his strength and speed.

Because he, too, felt the influence of the death-stone.

The buyer, ignorant and too eager to hold his new acquisition to heed the obvious signs that all was not well, gestured impatiently for the ugly bag. The man in possession of it picked up the bag, his expression sly and twisted, like a man who knew he was being paid to divest himself of trouble. He held it out—

The vampire stepped out of the shadows, said something short and low and commanding. *Demanding the bag!* Khundarr thought with horror. He wished these people no ill; he knew they were trying to help in their fumbling, ignorant way, but—

No matter the cost.

Things happened suddenly then. The vampire hesitated, his assurance suddenly rocked by the few steps he'd taken toward the stone; the stone surged in response, sucking in emotion, spewing it back out again, a distorted cyclonic funnel of what had once been the fine, crisp impressions of a warrior's death. The emanations bludgeoned the vampire, a shock wave of emotions that slammed into every demon within the confines of this zoo. A low moan rose around the building, a myriad of demons pushed to insanity, voicing their pain in chirps and snarls and growls and ululations that no human ear was meant to hear.

The buyer grabbed the stone and leaped for escape.

The Tuingas leaped to stop him.

The rest of the demons just plain leaped.

CHAPTER FIFTEEN

Angel staggered under the onslaught of the stone. Vaguely aware that his friends battled for their lives, he could do nothing to help. He fell to his knees, losing even the control to stay on his feet as Angelus within him surged to meet the anger and hatred and insanity beating against him from without.

Let go. Embrace it.

Cordelia cried out from behind him—surprise or pain, he couldn't tell, and couldn't do so much as look to see.

Give up.

"I won't," he said to that self inside himself, speaking through clenched teeth . . . hanging on.

But he couldn't break free either.

A shriek of fear penetrated the cacophony, and then a shriek of death. An instant later, one of the Tuingas flung the body of the buyer onto the terrace, a limp bundle of bones. Even in death the man clutched the bowling bag handles—but the bag ripped open, and the exposed stone skidded free. From his other hand, a knife pinwheeled toward Angel across the ground.

A misshapen lump of a demon with several sets of arms appeared and launched itself at the Tuingas; they fell and rolled down the hill, crashing through the carefully tended landscaping. Demons loomed everywhere; Wesley shouted a warning to Gunn, and Angel—the only still figure in the middle of a barbarous melee—struggled to respond. To help.

"Angel!" Cordelia cried, eluding a trio of demons who were doing their best to devour one another. She took shelter up against a palm, immediately striking up the strategy of *don't-notice-me*. But Angel didn't even seem to hear her cry for backup. He just swayed there, on his knees, his face twisted with his conflict and the offending stone only a few feet away.

She wanted to smash it into little bits, but didn't think it would be that easy. She still wanted to *try*—but there was the small matter of getting there. Wesley and Gunn fought with grim determination, unable to do anything but slash and duck, evading one lethal attack just in time to face another. They double-teamed a Miquot, keeping it too busy to grab its own homegrown knives with the short, curving *jambiyas* Cordelia had flung them. She still had the satchel, and the satchel still had weapons, but . . .

She didn't even know where to start.

They needed Angel.

Join them, whispered a maniac voice within him. But it referred to the demons, not to his friends. Angel closed his eyes and said, more loudly than before, "I *won't*."

And though he trembled with the effort, he still couldn't break free—couldn't find the strength to shut out the emanations that drew Angelus so close to the surface, and could barely find the strength to keep that evil riff of laughter from rippling out of the body Angelus called home.

When two whirling, catfighting demons slammed into him, it sent him sprawling. His concentration shattered, but with the stone only inches from his face, even Angelus lay stunned. A moment later, Lutkin's headless body toppled over Angel's back, and an unfamiliar voice cried a warning:

"Watch out!"

The faux Angel?

Lutkin's body lifted from Angel's legs, smashed into the side of the building, and sprawled at a grotesque angle along both ground and wall.

Rough hands of a berserker demon grabbed him next, lifted him, prepared to throw him—

A strange, determined scream filled the air, and Angel, dangling, recognized it as a battle cry from a throat that had never before sounded any such thing. Dropped, he thudded back to the ground, those same inches away from the stunning emanations of the stone. An instant later, David Arnnette smashed into the side of the building and slid down to rest on top of Lutkin . . . a sacrifice.

To protect Angel.

Finally, the faux Angel understanding what it was all about to be Angel. Finally, doing the right thing. And it stirred something in Angel that had been frozen under the deathstone assault, something that remembered the pain of Slith poison and how it had freed him. The pain of the war dart, inadvertent but just as effective. And he reached an unsteady hand for the buyer's discarded knife, a fanciful thing with an inlaid hilt and a sweeping designer blade and patently cheap metal.

But as his fingers closed around the hilt, that same rough berserker grip closed on his shoulder and his leg, lifting him—

Khundarr cried a wordless protest as one of his priests roared in pain . . . and melted away. It was little satisfaction to know that the lowest of underpriests waited in safety, prepared to swiftly collect any deathstones this night should produce. Khundarr himself, dripping ichor from a dozen small wounds, snarled at the three demons who had pushed him up against a wall. He impaled one of them, disemboweled another, and faced down the third—but his attention was on the center of the fray, where the hotel's vampire had come face-to-face with the stone, another demon looming over him.

Khundarr's hope sank away. This vampire had shown himself to be an ally, if an ignorant one—but no demon-blooded creature could come so close to touching an unstable deathstone and remain sane. And this vampire, insane, could not be allowed possession of the stone—for he had the strength and knowledge and cunning to turn the fight against the Tuingas, to deny them the stone altogether. To use it, while he could, to sow destruction in this world.

For the warrior's sake, Khundarr could not allow that to happen. For the sake of all those living here, he could not allow that to happen.

He had to reevaluate his strategy. To reassess his determination to return the warrior's stone to his people, where the most skilled of priests would heal it, and sneezing young Tuingas would be allowed nowhere near it. With the vampire so near the stone, and so obviously near the edge of his sanity, there was no other choice.

Destruction of the stone.

Khundarr absently blinded the third demon and shoved it away. Immediately he crouched down, making himself less of a target for those numerous demons still crowding into the area, those looking for something—*anything*—to kill, whether such behavior was natural to them or not. It put him in the perfect position to see two hapless zoo attendants rush into Zoo Meadow below, responding to the great trumpeting calls of the housed elephants and the racket of the great apes beyond. They hesitated, gaping uphill at the terrace. At the crest of the hill, right out front, the humans from the hotel fought like a team—dispatching demons, covering one another's backs, knowing one another's strengths and weaknesses. Even so . . . they were slowing. They'd all taken injuries. The woman limped, the white man was splotted with blood, and the black man protected his ribs. Dead demons encircled them, piling up close—hemming them in, but also making it much harder for the next wave of demons to close on them.

Khundarr silently bid the keepers to silence, but telepathy was not one of the Tuingas's gifts. The keepers stood in aghast speechlessness for only a moment, and then spoke rapidly into handheld devices, a hysterical note making their overlapping voices shrill and panicked.

The sound of prey.

The keepers didn't actually have the chance to say much, not once the rioting demons noticed them. A tragedy, the death of those without the immortality of deathstones.

And there was only one way to stop it. Khundarr returned his attention to the center of the battle . . . and to the warrior's stone.

Whatever the cost.

Just a thread of thought, that's all Angel had left. An intent, loosed from his mind like an arrow and set free in his body. His fingers curled around the knife. His mind, battered by the deathstone, battered by the parts of himself he fought so hard to keep buried, remained almost unaware of that arrow of intent, that one last supreme effort to win this inner battle even as his demon attacker lifted him right off the ground, hefting him—

Fingers, curled around the knife hilt. Clutching it.

He jammed the blade home in his own arm.

Pain slashed through his body, sharp and piercing. Undeniable. It cut away the surging influence of the deathstone, making his perceptions abruptly sharp and clear.

Demons surrounded his friends, fighting out of madness. The Tuingas were here; one had died not far from him. And Angel himself . . .

. . . felt his thoughts go fuzzy again, so close to

the deathstone. Its emanations coiled through his mind, distorting his emotions, reaching past his soul to call to Angelus . . .

He twisted the knife.

Pain sweet pain. He gasped, and didn't waste any more time. Twisting in the grip of the giant who held him aloft, he wrenched free, flipping in midair to land on his feet. He used what was left of his momentum to add strength to the blow that drove the knife through the demon's eye.

It didn't much faze the demon at all; the creature backhanded him up against one of the fish tanks. Something cracked at the impact; everything hurt. "Pain is good," he reminded himself out loud, adjusting his grip on the gory knife. Blood dripped down his arm; it was a worse wound than anything the demons had done, and would not heal quickly. "Pain is *sanity*."

Infuriated in its deathstone-driven rage, the demon roared like a posturing wrestler in a temper, squinching its face up to bellow with the entire considerable strength of its lungs. When it straightened to attack, opening its eye to search for its presumably stunned prey, Angel was waiting. The knife punched through the socket of that remaining eye, up to the hilt and even a little beyond.

Blinded and beside itself, the demon swatted at him; Angel jerked the knife back with a nasty sucking sound and said with some disbelief, "There's gotta be a brain there *somewhere*—"

Or not, because the demon targeted in on his voice and flung him back across the terrace to leave blood trails down the glass side of another colorfully inhabited aquarium. Angel staggered to his feet. "Pain is good," he insisted to himself, wiping blood out of his eye in a futile effort that only left his vision smeared. "Really. Just this once . . ." He blinked fiercely, certain the huge demon would follow the sound of his impact against the glass but unable to see just where—

Another blink, and suddenly he could see all too clearly. The demon had followed not the sound of Angel versus aquarium but the sounds of three exhausted humans still doing battle. Three exhausted and inattentive humans, distracted by a skirmish downhill. Many of the other demons had rushed downhill to join in; it sounded like a feeding frenzy. The blinded demon lumbered at them, picking up momentum . . . Angel flung himself after it, knife raised and aiming this time for the base of the skull—

Except that when Gunn glanced over, a *jambiya* in one hand and the jagged handle of a broken battle-ax in the other, his gaze stopped at Angel; his eyes widened considerably. Wesley whirled, raising his own weapon; Cordelia looked over and gave a faint shriek of horror. In that moment,

Angel knew just what they saw: a crazed and bleeding vampire, coming in for the kill. To kill *them*. And Gunn stepped out before the other two, raising the broken ax handle. Ready.

But the demon came on . . . and so did Angel. Not certain who would reach who first, but unable to break away. *Unwilling*.

Cordelia gave a shout—she'd seen the demon. Gunn hadn't—*couldn't,* as long as he locked his gaze on Angel—and yet something seemed to change. A resolve in his expression, a determination that *he* would not be the one to do this thing. He pulled the ax handle back, and his expression turned to a different kind of astonishment as Angel launched himself off the small pile of bodies in front of Gunn and barreled into the demon directly in front of the group, burying the knife in the back of its skull, hunting some small remnant of a brain stem.

It only made the demon mad.

"That's not right," Angel said. "That's just really not right." And as the demon groped for the knife jammed into the back of its head, Angel aimed a kick of utter frustration at its backside and knocked it out cold.

"I suppose that answers that question," Wesley said, aiming for a tone of driest English wit and only managing to sound tired.

"Which question?" Gunn asked, looking from Angel to the demon as Angel surreptitiously closed a hand around his bleeding arm, going for the look of someone holding a wound while he prodded it into fresh pain, driving away the deathstone from the edge of his thoughts. "Whether Angel is really trying to kill me, or whether you can ever again ask someone if they're sitting on their brains and think you actually know the answer?"

"Both, I think," Cordelia said, pushing her hair back and probably entirely unaware of the ichor with which she'd just slimed herself. But then her eyes widened in alarm, and Angel whirled to see a demon slinking for the deathstone, moving like a ghostly gecko and far too close to success—

Angel dove for it. For the demon or the stone, he wasn't sure—he just knew one couldn't get control of the other even as he dreaded getting close to the stone again.

From the darkness beyond the terrace, a Tuingas charged them both. Heavy-bodied, stout-necked, the odd throat-nose swinging with his motion. Wait—not charging *them*. Charging for the deathstone. Diving outstretched from thick splayed fingers to flat feet, the fresh and familiar scar tissue on his chest shiny in the garish purple light of the aquariums.

As Angel collided with the gecko-demon, the Tuingas closed his hands around the stone.

The darkness turned to brilliant day as the terrace rocked with a sharp explosion, a sudden clap of thunder from the very center of a storm. No one stayed afoot, not the demons, not the humans. Angel skidded back against a hard wall, arms flung up to protect his face and eyes, a flash of instinctive fear at such strong light against his skin.

The light faded; his ears rang in the silence. An odd stench filled the air.

The emanations were gone.

Even as Wesley, Cordelia, and Gunn climbed to their feet, helping one another up and then leaning against one another in an unsteady way, the demons began to regain their senses, to realize they didn't want to be here in this very public place, drawing attention to themselves with this very public slaughter. Not even the Miquot cared to focus such attention on themselves. As silently and swiftly as possible, they slunk away.

Angel, too, slowly regained his feet, his eyes recovering enough to find the spot where the deathstone had lain, deadly and pulsing. *Had* lain, for it was gone, now. A short distance away was a new deathstone, patently different in size, shape, and color; there was no goo in evidence. With dazed understanding, Angel said, "He knew that would happen. . . ."

"What?" asked Cordelia.

"When the Tuingas . . . priest . . . touched the stone, it caused a—"

"Big bang," Cordelia concluded on her own. "Not *the* big bang, but you know . . . it felt close."

"Careful," Gunn warned.

But Angel had seen it. Another Tuingas. A smaller version, hesitant but determined-looking. Easing in from the darkness with wary caution, heading for the new stone. Angel took a deliberate step back. "This one's all yours," he said.

"Please," said Cordelia.

"Be our guest," Gunn added.

"Now would be good," Wesley said as the Tuingas continued to watch them. Finally it darted in, grabbed the stone and, with a strange sucking noise, spiraled into . . . elsewhere. Its pocket dimension.

They stood alone among the purple-limned wall aquariums and the palms, marked by blood and surrounded by gore, the air still singed with the smell of burnt Tuingas flesh.

Gunn gave a deeply conspicuous sniff. "Ahh," he said with gusto. "The *other* white meat."

CHAPTER SIXTEEN

Gunn went down the line of kids, shaking hands, clapping shoulders . . . bumping fists. Eleven of them had stuck it out until last night—more than he'd thought would do. And all eleven of them had stuck it out *through* the night.

He couldn't help the silly grin that kept sneaking itself onto his face.

"We did good, huh?" Sinthea said, arching one of her fabulous brows and flipping her sleek black hair over one shoulder. She sported a clinging, low-cut top with flower embroidery, subtly applied makeup, and a variety of ugly bruises.

"You did," Gunn agreed. Around them, sunshine washed across MacArthur Park, a pleasant and easy-to-live-in day with the totally out-of-place signs of crazed demon activity all around them. Broken branches, dried blotches of no-one-wants-to-know, chunks of torn pavement . . . on Wilshire, a car still rested on its roof, a trail of paint and scrape marks tracing the spinning path it had taken before coming to rest up against the curb. Elsewhere, the discarded detritus of an EMT team marked their swift departure and overworked condition. Gunn hadn't heard a final death toll yet, but initial numbers were much lower than he'd feared. The rampaging demons had been so far gone, they hadn't been able to follow up on the trouble they started; except for those at the zoo, the night evening had been full of *hit and run* rather than *search and destroy*.

At the zoo, patrons had fled to be treated for mass hysteria while newly sane demons had cleaned up after their own, a process that started even as the gang limped for the exit—an exit still open by virtue of the tram that had been abandoned right there in the gateway. David Arnnette and Lutkin, they'd left behind. The logistics of hauling them around aside, leaving them there to be discovered and cared for, was the best option available. They'd be identified, their next of kin would be notified . . . and if the cause of their deaths was never explained, those mysteries would only be one of many from this night.

"Good enough to carry this demon watch thing our own way now?" Sinthea challenged Gunn, pulling him back to the here and now. The line broke as watch members shifted closer, expressions attentive. They were a mismatched crew, with young men who wouldn't get their full growth for years, and young women from the stick end of the spectrum . . . and the Sinthea end of the spectrum. They ranged from blond to Tyree's deepest black, and as far as Gunn knew, spoke five different languages among them. At least five. All of them come together—truly working together—around the single focus point he'd provided.

Himself.

He eyed them all and drawled, "Yeah, why not carry it on your own? Because you've been doing it for so long now, after all."

She grinned, no resentment in it. "It was worth a try. But hey, Gunn—no worries. After last night . . . you know, I really don't think I want to rush it."

A jogger ran by their little gathering, pretending not to see it. No doubt he'd had a lot of practice in pretending not to see things today already. They were merely a group of kids gathered after school. A bruised and battered group of kids who last night had learned to run when they were told to, to stand back when they were told to . . . and so hadn't lost anything but a little blood.

"No point in rushing it," Gunn said. "Besides—you work slow and steady, by the time you get to the really big stuff, the big stuff has heard of you and moved away. Gone somewhere else to cause trouble."

"90210," suggested Sinthea, and got a big laugh for it.

Gunn grinned right along with her. And then he got more serious, and he said, "All the same . . . you've proven you know where to start, and that you'll stick to the plan. There's gonna be days I'm taking care of other things . . . you'll be on your own a lot of the time." And then, in case they hadn't gotten it, he added, with just the slightest emphasis, "Sticking to the plan."

Sinthea exchanged a quick smile with Tyree. Tyree wasn't saying much today . . . not with that impressively lumpy and bruised jaw. But he nodded, and Sinthea said, "We'll stick to the plan just fine. I guess we've learned that much from watching you."

"Is he awake?" Gunn asked as he entered Caritas, swinging out of the way of a small demon who scuttled out into the early evening darkness it had been waiting for. Cordelia nodded toward a cluster of tables and continued sweeping paper debris toward the black plastic garbage bag in the center of the room. In the far corner quivered the cloak demon, separated from its host by the shock waves of the previous night and too baffled by the no-violence injunction on the lounge to do anything about finding another, more appropriate symbiont.

"Oh, I'm awake," Lorne said, emerging from

beneath the table with cleaning solution in hand. Instead of a suit jacket, he wore an artist's smock of deepest maroon with lime green piping. It only emphasized the bloodshot nature of his already brilliant red eyes; whatever protection the pitcher had held, it clearly came with a price.

Gunn winced. "Man," he said. "Whoever made that for you . . . you didn't pay them nearly enough."

"It was a gift," Lorne said dryly, and his voice rose with much meaningful emphasis as he added, "from someone who *appreciates* me."

"Hey, we appreciate you," Angel said, his voice drifting down from the top of a very high ladder as he applied a scrub brush to the wall, trying to remove Cordelia didn't want to know what. The natural job for the hang-around-on-the-rooftops guy he was. Not so natural for a guy still favoring his arm from his own horrible self-inflicted wound, but Angel hadn't really wanted to talk about that part. Hadn't even let Cordelia play nurse, and since they all knew he'd heal pretty much just as well anyway, they let it go. But she knew . . . if it was still on the tail end of healing nearly twenty-four hours later, it had been a nasty thing.

She remembered the business with the war dart and knew he'd done it to keep hold of his sanity. And she couldn't imagine doing it herself . . . but then, she couldn't imagine holding an inner demon like Angelus at bay either. She'd teased him about Tom Cruise and Harrison Ford and their heroic qualities . . . but really, she knew who the hero was here.

As long as he kept Angelus under wraps.

Belatedly, she said, "Of course we appreciate you, Lorne."

"See?" Angel said, with the kind of *so there* tone in his voice as if they'd all jumped up and showered acclaim on Lorne.

"No kidding," Lorne said flatly. "Then why is it every time I'm cleaning up a mess, your little gang is always around?" He gestured broadly at the club, into which desperate demons had crammed themselves as though it were some sort of bomb shelter. In a way, Cordelia supposed it was. Those who wanted to be safe were; those who wanted to keep themselves from acting under the influence of the deathstone did.

But exceeding the code capacity so outrageously had left its mark.

"Whose little gang?" Gunn asked. Cordelia knew he had his own little gang going now—well, not *gang* gang, but that bunch of kids he'd been talking about since the night before, how they'd done this and that and of course had watched the hotel and, most of all, had finally realized the wisdom of doing things his way. Cordelia had finally adopted a polite nodding strategy for these moments, but only after blunt discouragement had failed to work.

"Yes," Wesley said, looking up from the stage equipment, where he'd no doubt been wishing Fred had felt more prepared to venture out and apply her considerable brainpower to the malfunctioning bits. "I wondered that myself."

Lorne hesitated long enough to tell Cordelia he'd meant Angel's little gang, but he apparently recalled it wouldn't go over so well anymore, so when he responded, it was to say firmly, "*This* little gang. And don't change the subject. You know I'm right." He leaned down to pull a chair to its feet only to discover that it rocked significantly from one diagonal pair of legs to the other. He shoved it up against the table leg to steady it, and moved on to the next one.

"Hey," Angel said, turning on the ladder in such a precarious manner that it made Cordelia want to run over and steady the bottom rungs. "This one wasn't ours. We didn't do it . . . we fixed it."

Lorne snorted, unappeased. "But the misguided young man who let things get so messy was imitating you."

Cordelia winced—and she thought the ladder really would tip this time. It might have, if Angel hadn't abandoned his perch by the expedient method of simply jumping to the floor, taking that first step like it was nothing and landing with only the slightest of crouches. The look on his face was entirely wounded, and she found herself wondering when in his evolution—because she wasn't sure one could call it a life—he'd begun to care so much what his friends thought.

Since when had he had friends? The question came unbidden to her mind. After all, he'd been no prize before Darla sired him into Angelus; he'd said as much himself. And Angelus . . . evil like that had no friends, just enemies-to-be. But she looked at his face again and knew that he did care, and found herself saying rather suddenly, "No, he wasn't—imitating Angel, I mean. He had it all wrong."

"Except for that bit at the end," Wesley said unexpectedly.

"You mean the part where he got himself killed," Angel said flatly.

"That was his own doing," Wesley said. "His own decisions and his own behavior put him in that spot. One might consider him lucky for having the chance to make that one heroic gesture before he died. Somewhere along the way, you seem to have made quite an impression on him."

They turned to him, universally aghast.

Wesley winced. "Let's just pretend I didn't say that."

"Let's," Lorne said in his driest possible tone.

But Cordelia thought Wesley had it right.

• • •

The Tuingas elderpriest walked slowly toward the shrine, crunching on a soothing stick of rolled and dried latex tree bark. An expensive import from the anchor dimension, but well worth it for its contemplation-inducing nature.

Beside him walked an under-priest, silent and a little cowed. The elderpriest might have tried to counsel his underling out of the mood had he not felt the priest had plenty to be cowed about. The only survivor of the recent great unpleasantness had witnessed the results of a deathstone gone wild, and watched his fellow team of priests succumb to crazed demons. He'd watched the senior team leader sacrifice himself, throwing his own body over the deathstone to create the contact that destroyed them both . . . unstable deathstone and living Tuingas flesh.

But the young under-priest himself had brought back the results of that heroic act: Khundarr's deathstone, complete with the impressions of his last moment . . . the determination, the certainty, even the peacefulness success had brought him. In a rare and subtle echo, impressions from the warrior's stone—the initial impressions, undistorted and cherished—made themselves known.

Together, the priests entered the shrine that held Khundarr's stone. Marble-faced, simply appointed, a quietly stark chamber meant to pull a visitor's focus to the pedestal in the middle. It had once held the warrior's stone; now Khundarr's stone sat upon it, offering visitors the carefully protected and prepared memories of both heroes.

Off to the side, in one of the many wall niches, the first secondary stone resided. Much smaller, from a less imposing individual. The young Tuingas whose untimely doublesneeze had set the entire crisis in motion. Rather than revile the young one and his stone, they had chosen to acknowledge his honor and bravery, and his attempts to set things right.

Before they went any closer, the elderpriest removed from his sash pocket an object newly incorporated into the ritual of shrine visits: a squeezably soft bottle. "Here," he said to the under-priest, speaking for the first time since they'd embarked on this visit. "Partake deeply."

Reverently, the under-priest accepted the bottle, holding it in both hands before him as he prepared his long-nose, admiring the bright red and white label.

NASAL SPRAY. JUMBO SIZE.

CHAPTER SEVENTEEN

With Caritas mostly back in good order, and Lorne looking almost alert again and not the least bit chagrined at having ducked out of the worst of the trouble, Angel took the leisurely underground route back to the Hyperion and let the others cram themselves into the cab of Gunn's truck. Not that it was daylight—it wasn't—or that he couldn't have fit into the truck if he'd really wanted to. He simply found himself ready for some time alone.

After all, it hadn't been even a day since he'd been in the grips of a desperate struggle with himself. And he'd won—again—but it had been close enough to make him wonder if he always *would* win. The darkness within him seemed indefatigable . . . and the fight an unending one.

And he still didn't *get* it. David Arnnette and his misguided admiration and emulation, an emulation that had resulted in his own death. Something in Angel wanted to feel guilty about that, but mostly he thought Cordelia had the right of it . . . Arnnette had focused on the wrong things, had wanted the wrong things . . . and he'd paid for it.

As for Angel, he was already living his life the best he could. It was a life built on bad decisions and desperate moments, and he was lucky to have the chance to try to turn that around.

When he ambled into the Hyperion lobby, he found Cordelia and Fred engaged in a microwave popcorn–tossing competition, with Wesley and Gunn as their somewhat sheepish targets. Both men snapped their mouths closed as they noticed Angel; unperturbed, Cordelia and Fred switched to tossing popcorn at each other.

"I have this idea," Fred said, as a kernel bounced off her cheek. "A funnel thing, with a coating of just the right ionic balance to attract buttered popcorn. I'm just not sure . . . it seems like maybe the time is better spent on this other idea I have—"

"I kinda think a funnel thing with an ionic coating might take the *fun* right out of it," Cordelia said, tossing a kernel straight up in the air and stumbling backward, still stiff and awkward from all the close calls of the night before, to catch it in her open mouth. Which she did, but not until she'd bumped into Angel.

He steadied her, stole a piece of her popcorn, and aimed it at Fred. Fred caught it with undiluted glee, and Angel found himself smiling as he eased past Cordelia to the refrigerator behind the counter. *Just a little snack . . .*

"We figure it was one of their priests, all right," Wesley said, as if they'd all been talking business right along. No doubt he was entirely unaware of the little greasy blots of popcorn butter all over the front of his shirt. "It was certainly the same fellow you wounded the other night."

Angel leaned on the counter, picking up the new demon guide from which Cordelia had eventually gleaned the final crucial clues. By now it automatically opened to the section on Tuingas, with its obscure references to a pocket dimension tribe and the priests who oversaw the deathstones. "Probably he's a martyr among his people."

"Or a hero," Wesley agreed. "Too bad we weren't of much help. Not until the end, anyway, when we at least gave the other demons something to attack besides the Tuingas."

"Yeah," Gunn agreed, wiping his hands futilely across the stains on his own blocky, long-sleeved T-shirt. "But you gotta admit, those guys had stone—"

"Let it go, Gunn," Cordelia said, quick and hard, and aiming a meaningful look at him to boot.

"No way," said Gunn, not in the least deterred. "There are way too many good puns and double-entendres left."

"Use my office," Wesley suggested. "Go in there,

close the door, and just blurt them all out at once."

"It would be safer that way," Cordelia agreed. Beside her, Fred smiled the quiet but genuine smile she'd started to show them between the moments of obvious crisis that were standard operating procedure around the hotel.

Angel flexed his arm, thinking that it was a good smile, and thinking with any luck they'd avoid plunging into any new moments of obvious crisis for at least a day or two.

"Is it all right?" Fred asked, and Angel looked at her in confusion, still stuck in his thoughts. "Your arm, I mean," she added. "I couldn't believe it when Cordelia told me—"

"It's fine," Angel said hastily. His need to take such desperate means to keep his hold on Angelus wasn't something he wanted to dwell on. Self-consciously, he put the arm down on the front counter, setting his snack down in front of it. *No, wait, that wasn't any better, putting the blood right out there to remind them of the vampire thing which would only remind them of the Angelus thing* . . . Quickly, he moved it to the side.

But no one really seemed to notice any of it. They were pretty much suddenly lost in their own thoughts, their own experiences of the night before. Cordelia still limped, and Wesley had obvious bruises beneath the popcorn grease. A bandage peeped out from beneath Gunn's sleeve, and a cut had scabbed over his brow. They were all more than just a little bit lucky that the demons had in fact been so enraged that their capacity for thought—not to mention a canny fight—had deserted them entirely.

Angel had simply been lucky. Lucky to have found something that worked, lucky to realize it when the clues came his way.

As usual, Cordelia read him the best. "Not everyone would have had the—"

"Stones," Gunn supplied, unrepentant.

"—courage to do what you did," she said, taking no apparent notice of the interruption.

He knew where she was going with this one. "He chose the wrong role model."

"You've got that all figured out now?" she asked, one arched eyebrow suggesting that she didn't think so.

"Yeah," he said. "I think I do."

"So tell us," Wesley said. "You've been around a while. You've got more examples than most to choose from. So who . . . ?"

"My role models?" Angel asked, eyeing the popcorn smears and bruises and cuts and stiffness-hampered movement as they all shifted a little closer, waiting for the answer to this one. But for once they'd asked him an easy one. "That would be you guys," he told them, earning another of those smiles from Fred, this one of approval, and leaving them speechless as he headed for the stairs, for the quiet refuge of his rooms and what he hoped would be a deeply dreamless sleep. Because for now, he'd chased all the demons away; the only ones leaving impressions on him were the people he wanted there.

For now.

DORANNA'S BACK STORY

After obtaining a degree in wildlife illustration and environmental education, Doranna spent a number of years deep in the Appalachian Mountains, riding the trails and writing sci-fi and fantasy books, eleven of which have hit the shelves. She's moved on to live in the Northern Arizona Mountains, where she still rides and writes, focusing on classical dressage with her Lipizzan. There's a mountain looming outside her office window, a pack of dogs running around the house, and a laptop sitting on her desk—and that's just the way she likes it.

You can contact her at:
dmd@doranna.net
or
P.O. Box 31123
Flagstaff, AZ 86003-1123
(SASE, please)

or visit www.doranna.net.

Buffy the Vampire Slayer™

Giles (to Buffy): "What did you sing about?"

Buffy: "I, uh . . . don't remember. But it seemed perfectly normal."

Xander: "But disturbing. And not the natural order of things and do you think it'll happen again? 'Cause I'm for the natural order of things."

Only in Sunnydale could a breakaway pop hit be a portent of doom. When someone magically summons a musical demon named Sweet, the Scoobies are involuntarily singing and dancing to the tune of their innermost secrets. The truths that are uncovered are raw and painful, prompting the question, "Where do we go from here?"

Now, in one complete volume, find the final shooting script of the acclaimed musical episode "Once More, With Feeling." Complete with color photos, production notes, and sheet music!

The Script Book: Once More, With Feeling

Available now from Simon Pulse
Published by Simon & Schuster

BUFFY The VAMPIRE SLAYER™

ALL SINGING BY ORIGINAL CAST!

"ONCE MORE, WITH FEELING"

The Musical Episode Soundtrack

Includes complete versions of all songs from the acclaimed musical episode, performed by the *Buffy* cast.

Bonus tracks include score segments from three other acclaimed *Buffy* episodes ("Restless," "Hush" and "The Gift"), plus a demo track from "Once More, With Feeling" sung by *Buffy* creator, Joss Whedon, and wife Kai Cole.

NOW AVAILABLE ON COMPACT DISC EVERYWHERE

Aaron Corbet isn't a bad kid—he's just a little different.

On the eve of his eighteenth birthday, Aaron is dreaming of a darkly violent landscape. He can hear the sounds of weapons clanging, the screams of the stricken, and another sound that he cannot quite decipher. But as he gazes upward to the sky, he suddenly understands. It is the sound of great wings beating the air unmercifully as hundreds of armored warriors descend on the battlefield.

The flapping of angels' wings.

Orphaned since birth, Aaron is suddenly discovering newfound—and sometimes supernatural—talents. But not until he is approached by two men does he learn the truth about his destiny—and his own role as a liason between angels, mortals, and Powers both good and evil—some of whom are bent on his own destruction....

the
fallen

a new series by Thomas E. Sniegoski

Book One available March 2003

From Simon Pulse

Published by Simon & Schuster

ROSWELL™

ALIENATION DOESN'T
END WITH GRADUATION

Everything changed the day Liz Parker died. Max
Evans healed her, revealing his alien identity. But
Max wasn't the only "Czechoslovakian" to crash
down in Roswell. Before long Liz, her best friend
Maria, and her ex-boyfriend Kyle are drawn into
Max, his sister Isabel, and their friend Michael's
life-threatening destiny.

Now high school is over, and the group has
decided to leave Roswell to turn that destiny
around. The six friends know they have changed
history by leaving their home.

What they don't know is what lies in store...

Look for a new title every other month from
Simon Pulse—the only place for *all-new*
Roswell adventures!

SIMON PULSE
Published by Simon & Schuster